# A GOD OF HUNGRY WALLS

# GARRETT COOK

deadite
press

deadite
press

DEADITE PRESS
P.O. BOX 10065
PORTLAND, OR 97296
www.DEADITEPRESS.com

AN ERASERHEAD PRESS COMPANY
www.ERASERHEADPRESS.com

ISBN: 978-1-62105-195-4

Printed in the USA.

*To the Houses,*
*Each of Them Haunted*

# HOMECOMING

The girl who left won't make it out of this alive. I taught her about love you see, and now she knows too much. The girl who left will not make it out of this alive. She knows too much about love. With nightfingers under the covers and breath in the ear, I taught her. Secret shape pressed against her, I was warm and I was tender, I was kind. You may say that I was cruel—am cruel—will always be cruel but you cannot tell me ever EVER that I wasn't kind or that kindness isn't in my nature. Although she used herself 'til blood sprayed and made white sheets a little rusty brown (a virgin with white sheets, imagine that) although I made sheets a rusty brown, although I cracked her open, let her out, I was kind. But she will not make it out of this alive. Who does?

The chill is back. Subtle right now. She is thinking of Ray Bradbury. I don't know the name. I'm with her at the pharmacy as she takes in the not quite food smell of candy corn, inhales bittersweet. The plastic pumpkin pail gets her wet. Reminds her of me. She really doesn't want to look at the plastic pumpkin pail, but I am in her. And when I get in you, I get in you. I am in deep. This thing is mine. It's better she won't get out of this alive. She knows too much about love.

She's on her knees last year.

"You want a treat?" I'm shaking a plastic pumpkin pail. Tempting her with candy corn and Necco wafers.

She nods and opens wide.

She turns, startled by an inflatable ghost looking at her with big, googly stupid eyes. She thinks of me, but not fondly. The girl who left leaves this place emptyhanded.

She walks to the train station past a street musician that she swears is me and she's not quite right and she's not quite wrong. She knows too much about love. She turns up her Ipod. It's playing our song. I would miss the girl who left if I had gone away.

"Imagine me and you, we two…"

Happy Together. The Turtles. She loved the song, even before it was ours. She scrolls down the playlist, switching to the next track.

"That I'm the only one for you, and you for me…"

She closes her eyes and insists that she's out and that she never never never ever…

"So happy together."

She always loved Sylvia Plath. She read me some poems. I wasn't sure that I could quite relate. I am never vulnerable. But that's why she's thinking about the oven. And the gas and getting out of this. Not alive. She knows too much about love.

Daddy, you bastard, I'm through. Don't think about the pumpkin pail.

She's going home to turn on the oven. And the girl who left is coming back home to me.

# INHABITANTS

Micah is up early. Sitting in the backyard meditating. He is listening to the trees, the plentiful trees, the great canopy of Jamaica Plain's Emerald Necklace. A short walk to the center of town, a short walk from the pond, still in isolation, still in stillness. An ideal place for this house, for him, for me. He is listening to the trees and I am whispering through them. It's a good idea to take in another. They had failed to fill the room the last couple months and their hearts are still heavy with the girl who left, but yes, it is the time. The Emerald Necklace has spoken, ground and leaves and wind.

He goes inside and brews his morning coffee in the kitchen, the only space where you can see the sum of who lives here. This is the only room where one might find any of them at once or all of them at once. Symbols of ancient mysticism, cartoon characters and pithy female empowerment slogans adorn the refrigerator, stickers and slogans paper the cabinets with liberation and love and light and lies, sigils of commitment to being better people than any of them are.

Kaz, in boxer shorts and black tanktop, is seated at the table. Micah looks up and down Kaz's body, a dancer's body, curved and strong in all of the right places, he tries not to let on that his gaze is one of longing. But he likes her Mohawk, he likes her eyes, he likes the way her breasts strain against her shirt, he likes her legs. He likes her big blue eyes. She likes him too, his long, blonde curly hair, his tan, his shirtless, unshod relaxed persona.

They want each other and are scared that it might happen, but today they aren't thinking about that for long. The girl

7

who left is dead and they finally found someone to take the room she left behind two months ago before she moved away and before she ended her life. The upstairs room in the corner, the Blue Room, as they refer to it, since its walls are a cerulean blue.

"I think it's gonna be cool," says Kaz, "the new guy seems nice. And he's a musician. You play guitar. You guys could jam. He's written stuff for commercials and singers and stuff. He knows his shit."

Micah nods.

"Yeah. He's a good dude. I like him."

"Yeah."

"You're up early."

"Late," says Kaz.

"Ah."

Leah walks shyly into the kitchen. Pours hot water into her French press.

"Good morning," she says, almost inaudibly. Though thin and graceful, darkhaired and beautiful, envied by Kaz for her Chinese exoticism, her posture is small, her body language protected. She is cocooned in her oversized sweatshirt, hiding her bust, hiding her size as she often tends to. She is surprised to see Kaz up this early, though for Kaz it is probably late instead, she may be a couple hours before seeing bed and waking up at three o' clock. Kaz tends to be nocturnal, which is fine for Kaz. Leah isn't judging, even though she is. Though nowhere near as harshly as she judges herself.

"Brian is moving in today."

"Cool," says Leah.

Micah feels her unease but isn't sure where it comes from. She wasn't around when Brian met the others but she'd said that was okay and mostly Leah kept to herself. So, it was probably okay. But Leah still seems uneasy and Micah doesn't like that. Micah tries to keep the household running smoothly. He is a man of action and above the stereotypes about people like him. At least that's what he tells himself. At least that's what he seeks to prove. So, Micah doesn't like Leah's unease.

"You're okay with this, right?"

Leah had liked the girl who left. Micah had seen the two of them together sometimes. Micah hopes this doesn't mean she'll be rude to the new guy but Leah doesn't seem to be rude to anyone. She keeps to herself, which is fine, except that nobody likes it. Everyone tends to feel she thinks she's better than they are.

"Yeah," says Leah, "if you guys think he's okay, he's probably okay."

Kaz can't help but laugh.

"Yeah, probably. Barring some massive oversight, I guess."

"He's fat," says Micah, "and a racist. He's a big fat racist."

Cytherea waddles into the kitchen. Seeing this bloated beast reminds me why he ogles Kaz. She is a skilled, insatiable lover but generally cruel and crude. As usual, she's all gut and tit and ass and dresses in a generally whorish manner. Right now it is just a long, black men's t-shirt emblazoned with Blessed Be, which is a laugh. Generally seems her spells don't work any better than the weights she sporadically lifts. Or maybe they do. It might explain how a fat purplehaired slut in far too much makeup picks up a man as attractive as Micah and manages to bring home as many lovers as she does.

"You talking about the new guy? I hear he's a Satanist."

Leah has no idea why Cytherea would think it would frighten her if he was a Satanist or why it would be funny. She wants Leah to be shocked because that would make her look cool in front of Kaz and Cytherea always wants to look cool in front of Kaz. There is really no place Cytherea would be cool.

"He's hot. I'm gonna suck his cock," says Kaz.

"I'm gonna suck it first," counters Cytherea. Cytherea is only half joking, just as Kaz is not joking at all. Kaz would not mind sucking his cock. Cytherea will try to make it happen. Though Cytherea thinks of herself as an ethical slut and Kaz as a regular slut, Kaz is actually shyer, sadder, but less desperate in her way, less hungry. Literally too.

Micah waves his hands in mock protest.

"Whoa, whoa, let's not count Leah out yet. She's the dark horse in the race but she might surprise you."

Leah forces a smile.

"I rove him rong time," she deadpans.

She doesn't laugh and joke with them often but she wants them to be on her side because the new one is an unknown quantity. They laugh with her. They sit in the kitchen and eat breakfast together. They act like a family, like they know what a family is at all.

"He'll be into that," says Kaz, "total racist. You can seduce him with your subtle geisha ways."

"I will definitely give Leah subtle."

"Like a ninja," Micah chimes in.

"Racist," says Leah.

"You want half of my bagel? I'm trying to cut out some carbs," Kaz gestures toward Leah with half a bagel.

"I'm cutting out carbs too." Leah is telling a half truth. She's cutting out a lot more than carbs.

"You look fine," says Micah, "you should be careful. Nobody wants you getting sick."

Leah thinks on the subject. Thinks about the time she's spent eating nothing, talking to nobody, hiding in her room with her grief and her anxiety. She looks around for anybody who she assumes would care if she got sick and she finds nobody among these people, who are always too wrapped up in themselves and their things to so much as ask how she's doing. Julie was closest to her. Julie was her friend and they never stop and ask how she feels about her friend being gone.

"I'm okay," she replies, "really. I know about diet and stuff. I'm a med student after all."

"Really?" says Kaz "'Cause you never bring it up."

"Fuck that Cosmo shit," says Cytherea, "you look good in the body that's yours. Any body can be sexy."

Micah really wishes she would lose weight. Micah wants to know what's under Leah's baggy sweaters. Micah would have a lot of fun with that. Any body can be sexy but hers? No, not hers. She is not nearly so secure as she lets on. But she has to be so she lays it on real thick.

"I know that," says Leah, "I just want to be healthy."

That's a funny word in this house.

# THE NEW ONE

The new one, Brian—his hair and beard are long and I cannot glean his secrets straight away. He comes in part because there's already a bed, already a desk, already a room. Brian comes with three suitcases and a couple of boxes of equipment that he has placed in the basement. He will spend a great deal of time in the basement.

The basement is full of memories. It is full of Antonia. It is full of Maddy and Clarence. It is full of me. The new one has set up his things but he is settling in and has not yet come down there. I will get to know him quicker when he does. I have been tapping the glass on his window, waking him in the middle of the night. His ears are keen since he's a musician.

That much I know. I don't know all that much more yet. At this stage in our acquaintanceship, I feel like a goddamn child, pulling juvenile pranks to gain attention. But he will not get to know me if he ignores me. I look at him through Kaz and don't find out much. He is one of Kaz's types. Kaz cannot tell me much but she wants to take him to bed because he plays the guitar and has a beard.

I see desire and thirst for approval from Kaz's eyes so she doesn't help much. Kaz's desire is a gateway to Kaz and to nothing more than Kaz, this is true even for Kaz. She wants many things she doesn't want to remind herself that she wants at all. If she ever stopped wanting, that would be the end of her, though that could be said for most people I suppose.

This makes me want to reach him even more. So I push hard. His mind doesn't want me in there. It has no reason to.

I have given him nothing and he has no reason to trust me or trust the home. I need something though. He is making me a petulant child but I don't care. I want what I want. I hunger for what I hunger for. I am a hypocrite a bit for indicting Kaz.

I can smell that he is looking to forget. They will hang paintings on cracks in the wall. They will sweep piles of clutter into the closet. They will haphazardly toss sheets over careworn furniture as time and dust and vermin rot upholstery away. This one is in his way quite gifted, a prodigy, it seems, at the art of forgetting. I cannot find what I'm looking for because he can't.

Feeling my intrusion but unable to articulate what or where or why the not alone comes from, he pops open a beer. For a musician, he is not terribly relaxed. That's why he's not in a band. He tells me that. Why his collaborations don't last too long. He tells me that. His relationships seem weak too, vulnerable to the same things that wreck his musical collaborations. Antonia. Yes, Antonia will find a way. He's high strung and nervous, vigilant and detail-oriented.

But the beer in his hand is a talisman, one that keeps him from overthinking. Which he does. Such an overabundance of thoughts, still waters running deep as they say. His mind races from the taste of the beer, from the settling of the wood, things that make him take a glance backward. We must try not to glance backward, hence the beer. I wish he could glance backward to help me find exactly what I am looking for. When he pulls away the blankets from the paintings, he reveals more blankets beneath them or that the paintings were paintings of blankets.

He looks out into the hallway because he feels not alone. Leah, who seems nice enough, is coming up the stairs but that's not it. He hadn't even heard her on the bottom stair. I show him a short, still image to distract him and take in what he's made of. Like one of Doctorpuppet's Rorschach blots.

13

I give him a naked man, over four hundred pounds, body made of rolls and wrinkles, blemishes, boils and sores. He is wearing on his head the skull of a bull. On her knees in front of him, naked, with freckle-dotted skin and flaxen hair, is a girl of about ten years old. He is holding her head up by pigtails and is gagging her tiny mouth with his giant cock. There is no action, no motion, it is suspended in space, a snapshot of this moment of shame and pain and exploitation. I show it to him for long enough for him to think he saw it, then I splice it into his memory again. Lurking between moments, between glances, is the child's supplication. I remember testing Doctorpuppet with this one. Doctorpuppet got out of bed and went to the shower to masturbate and cry. Because Doctorpuppet was terribly sick in his head, a physician that could never have healed himself.

Brian neither showers nor masturbates. I'm not sure if this delights or disappoints me, to be honest. He simply sits alone, with his feeling of not aloneness fully intact and his feeling of not quite rightness and his feeling of uncertainty at what he witnessed. Brian chugs down his beer. He contemplates calling someone or knocking on Leah's door to offer one of his beers to her. But he looks at his watch and he sees that it is only 3:30. It's too early to be drinking and he doesn't want to make a bad impression. And she probably doesn't really drink anyway.

If she drank, she wouldn't drink beer at 3:30, that's for sure. Maybe he needs some food or some fresh air. I try to tell him that his face is crumbling off and there is something unspeakable underneath, but it is too soon for that. Yes, I am getting impatient. I don't know him well enough to convince him of this, so there was no reason for me to try and with a great deal of shame and annoyance and humiliation, I am ejected. He decides it would be a good time to take a walk. I don't have him nearly enough to follow him out.

And so instead, I check up on Leah, in her room with its

bare yellow walls, with only calendars of great works of art to make it look like she thinks of herself as a person. She's studying and listening to music, trying not to get carried away again and therefore not to get carted away again. She wouldn't want to end up back in the hospital. She says she likes her body. She says she's doing well enough. She says that a bowl of frozen yogurt or an episode of Project Runway isn't going to hurt her. She subvocalizes this too many times for her to count. As if she could eventually believe it. It will hurt you. Make you fat. Make you fail. She makes a well of self assurance as she takes in the names of veins or nerves of bones of arteries, of all the things that can break them down, the myriad maladies that she will have to know by heart. The facts slip in but she loses them if I tweak just a little.

I ask her about the new guy because Kaz has been so uninformative. I want to know what she thinks. She isn't mine completely but she could be. She thinks that he is somewhat handsome though too scruffy for her to taste though he isn't actually all that scruffy all things considered, not like those friends of Micah's. She is worried he will not pay his share of utilities and that he will make a giant mess of the kitchen and that he will have loud parties and that she will not be asked to come down and join him. When Kaz has friends over, she never invites her down. She never asks if she would like to watch a movie or something. Or to have dinner. But Leah doesn't have dinner very often. The banana on her desk is moldy and disgusting and oozing with fat. Mustn't eat that banana. And Brian won't invite her to dinner either. And Brian is too cool to talk to her and Brian wants to be left alone. Everyone in the house just wants to be left alone. And that suits Leah because Leah needs to study to become a doctor and Leah is good enough and almost almost thin enough to become a doctor.

She thinks she likes him anyway and that he seems nice. He'd be more likely to invite her to hang out or something than Kaz would. Her mind is slightly fuzzy. Her mind is full of affirmation and pre-med with a soupcon of trust. This soupcon of trust is pushing me out and so I must push back. It is easy for me to suggest it might be hot in here. Simple and sad and a bit patronizing but to tell that it is hot in here will certainly start her up. She therefore looks in the mirror at herself in baggy sweatshirt and the sweatshirt and her body start to merge. And they're lumping into one, indeterminate and bland and grey and shapeless as Leah herself. Who the hell is Leah to say she's anyone? To remove the Tufts sweatshirt and look once more on lumpy imperfection. Though she is tight and moonfleshed and taut from exercise, she is shapeless, she is grey inside herself. Is it hot enough to risk ridicule and reveal her grotesquerie? To reveal the blobs over blobs over blobs?

She'd talked about these things with the one who left. They were almost friends. They both had stuff in common, bad ideas. I flash her face before Leah's eyes and make her think back. I infuse the room with her. I scatter atoms in the air. I let her breathe in the scent. Alone. Fat. Uncomfortable. Nose filled with her friend. She needs to throw out the banana, so she tosses out the banana. The banana was oozing with fat and Leah is oozing with fat. She shouldn't take off the sweatshirt since she is too much like it.

She sits down on the bed, head between her knees. She wants to cry but she would never let herself as her father and her mother would never let her. She is stunned and she must sit and listen. I tell her she doesn't like her and that nobody does and that she isn't welcome in this place. She should always say nothing. She should study harder though she is good enough to get good enough and thin enough to do what she must. Kaz doesn't like her. Micah doesn't like her. There is no way Brian likes her. He is too cool to like her and she should simply remain alone. Alone with the mirror and alone with me.

Something happens next that I don't like. It's something that doesn't happen in this house. It isn't likely most days, it doesn't happen most days, but it does. There is a knock on Leah's door. This was unanticipated. I tell her not to answer it because nobody wants to see her but she answers it. Brian is standing outside.

"I know you gotta study and it's still kind of early, but do you maybe want a beer? Everybody is off doing their own things and I thought maybe you'd like some company."

A shaken, vulnerable Leah nods in agreement and Brian goes to get the beers. I hate this man.

# CHAMPAGNE

Antonia is reading her Bible again. It is no longer words but she wants to be good and obedient. At least she thinks she does. Is she pious or selfish? Is she looking to preserve or protect her herself or is the love of God in her? She asks these questions. I know the answers but I'm not going to tell her. She thinks she wants to feel these things inside her and know them to be the truth. She thinks she wants to love God and love Clarence and Maddy and that ought to be enough.

Come Sunday, she'll sit down in church and she'll act like it's enough and she is Clarence and Maddy's housekeeper. Does she feel the love of God in the minutes of Sunday fresh air and sunlight? One could not help but do so, could they? The Bible reminds her of Sunday and the need to be loving and to appreciate everything she has. I think I might help her.

"You have so many nice things," I tell her, "you have warmth and comfort. You have a lovely home and you have Clarence and Maddy who love you."

Antonia nods as piss begins to dribble down her bare thigh. She feels ashamed but then thinks of Maddy's soft and loving hands on her at bath time. It could be bathtime tonight. Proof enough that Clarence and Maddy love her, that God loves her and that I love her too. Her shame is gone and replaced by gratitude that she is safe inside this cage in Clarence and Maddy's lovely home where the wickedness and danger and corruption outside cannot touch her.

"I love you Maddy," says Antonia.

She might prefer Maddy to Clarence, even though so many of the long red streaks and stripes upon her back are courtesy of Maddy's moods. But Maddy is justified. Antonia does bad things sometimes and thinks bad thoughts that I often bring to Maddy and Antonia must be punished for them. I do not always bring the truth to Maddy, since the truth isn't what she wants.

She wants the whip, the razors to leap into her hand. She wants an excuse for another drink and another go at the grimecovered little whore in the cage in the basement. The Kitten. Clarence hasn't touched her all that often since The Kitten. The Kitten wants Clarence to herself. She conspires. They were going to kill her like the other one. But somehow Clarence changed his mind and has chosen to keep The Kitten, who is having thoughts about Clarence and is having thoughts about escaping.

And if she escapes, she will ruin all this and Maddy and Clarence will be punished. And everything will be lost. I project before her eyes the girl with no skin, body still young and tight as when Clarence used it and made it his but skullfaced, missing giant clumps of hair, mouth sewn shut, head still bleeding from when Clarence bashed it in before tossing her out in the woods. Maddy sees this and takes another drink and she picks up the whip and she storms out of the bedroom.

It's three in the afternoon and she's still wearing her nightgown, the nightgown that barely holds back her great, sagged flapping breasts and does nothing to hide the wrinkles upon her wattle like neck, or the cellulite and pimples on her thighs. She does not have to dress up or hide her shame from The Kitten. She feels a little self conscious undressed or half dressed in front of Clarence but The Kitten is kitten and therefore less than people. And doesn't much of the shame come from The Kitten? She should punish the Kitten for making her feel this way, like she is less than wife and less than woman.

She grabs the whip and grabs her bottle of wine and she heads down to see The Kitten. The Kitten has gotten scared and shat again. Why does The Kitten's shit always smell so rank? Why is its piss so salty? The Kitten is such a dirty, stupid creature. Why do they have to keep the foul thing around? She thinks back to the last one. Clarence could still have a couple days fun with it anyway. And they could always get a new one. This one isn't special. It's ugly. It's getting skinny even though she feeds it good. Skinny stinking Kitten. Making her feel fat.

"Hello, mother," says The Kitten because Clarence makes The Kitten call Maddy "mother," even though Maddy doesn't like it at all. Maybe Clarence does it because Maddy doesn't like it at all. Clarence should know better. He's a goddamn doctor.

"You fucking shat yourself again, you stupid whore," says Maddy.

"Mother, I am sorry."

"Sorry doesn't clean up the fucking shit in your cage. You know what you have to do."

Antonia gets down on her knees, praying silently for strength. I examine the situation and though I once again show her the First Girl, the dead girl, I know that she is going to get just that. I don't know how it will play out but I know she is finding that strength. Even though she is on her knees, picking up a glob of her excrement, trying not to smell it as she pops it into her mouth. She knows Maddy will get mad if she just swallows it right away, so as always she makes a show of chewing it, tasting it, savoring it.

"How does that taste?" Maddy asks.

Antonia knows the script. She knows very well, exactly what she needs to say and that she can't say it with tears in her eyes or any hesitation. If she hesitates or cries, Maddy will retaliate and if Maddy retaliates, things will only get more miserable. Maddy can be very cruel, though Antonia should still feel grateful to have her.

"It tastes good. It's all that I deserve."

"That's fucking right, you dumb whore." She whips Antonia's bared back hard. Then again. Line after line, streak after streak of blood appear under the lash. Antonia asks God to make her strong enough to take this, to let this forge her into something beautiful and mighty and hopefully to die this time, this time maybe she will die of this and be accepted into the kingdom of Heaven. She didn't used to think of Heaven so much but Maddy was sure it was so and Clarence is sure that Heaven awaits the virtuous who suffer to be free of sin, so she allows this, hoping to slip away into the next world.

But those are suicidal thoughts and life's a gift. Life is a gift from God. She clings to life and prays to herself that God will free her from these thoughts of death and give her the strength to appreciate Maddy's love and the fortitude to take on Clarence's. They cherish and love her and keep her soul pressed close to their hearts and they want her to be strong and good and beautiful and right for her place at the right hand of God when she finally dies and floats on up to Heaven.

"Break the bottle," I whisper to Maddy, "kill the little slut. She has plans. Clarence and her have plans."

She does not need to be told this twice. She knows it is probably so because Clarence barely touches her anymore and he comes down and puts his dirty hands on The Kitten all night, pinching its scrawny body, dirtying himself inside its sinful sinful cunt. The plan is clear and Maddy will need to be sharp and smart and reassert her space. Yes, kill it. Break the bottle and be done with it. Stab it dead.

"She's going to kill you now," I whisper to Antonia, "she's going to kill you and defile your corpse. She is not one of mine but in the house of the enemy. You need to survive now, you need to live for the glory of God, for my glory. You cannot give up the gift of life yet."

Maddy shatters the bottle, Antonia turns. And for a

moment, I make the First Girl creep up on Maddy, let her muffled choking sounds remind her of what she's done and remind her of a debt that's coming due. Maddy's attention shifts away from the bottle, and Antonia sleek and wildcat tough, determined, takes the bottle from her and stabs her. Pounces. I play back and forth the indignities, remind her of the shit in her mouth, let her look once more upon the terrible face of the First Girl.

She brings Maddy to the ground, kneeling over her triumphant, broken bottle in her hand at the ready, stabs again, then remembers again all the torture, the pain and indignity and the filth she tried to pretend was something ascetic. She can see the fat, naked monster underneath her and everything it's done to her and the debt that's coming due. She takes the broken bottle and she forces it into the wide, stinking angry flaps of Maddy. She makes a thrust, frothing up juices and blood, then another, then another as the behemoth struggles beneath her begging her to stop, invoking the name of God and also every other filthy rude name she can think and there are plenty, the goddamn slattern.

Antonia keeps going and she doesn't stop until Maddy stops moving and protesting, she doesn't stop until there is a great big puddle of blood and pussy brine collected between Maddy's legs and there is a glassy empty look in the eyes of her oppressor. So Antonia does the only thing that makes sense. She crawls away from this, away from the murder she was just forced to commit. She picks up the whip, gets down on her knees and prays for some guidance, some absolution.

# SESSION

If you have faith in the walls, I am god.

I need only trust to become the Lord of Forms.

Kaz is having one of her sessions with Doctorpuppet.

"I don't think you're a real doctor."

"Of course I am."

"I'm not sure if you're real."

"But I am a doctor."

Fear widens her blue eyes. They become perhaps too big, too clear. This is why men avert their gaze. They are afraid of what might happen. She practically swallows her bottom lip. Kaz wants to tell Doctorpuppet that she is falling in love with him. But she won't. She knows that will make him go. She should know he never will. He is at the moment the vessel of her faith, if I take him away, she has no reason to believe. She should understand that nobody really leaves.

"I'm not going to ask her that," Doctorpuppet tells me, "it wouldn't be right. I don't like this."

You shut your jowly face. Nobody cares what you like. Nobody cares about your big bald head, your sad, canine mouth or your grey weepy eyes. You shut your jowly face or I'll make you hurt.

If you have faith in the walls, I am god. Doctorpuppet's a believer. I'm the first thing he believed in. Which makes me as vast as the sky. Doctorpuppet will behave. Doctorpuppet had been pious in the eyes of all around him, Doctorpuppet was an exemplary member of the community. But I was the first thing Doctorpuppet ever believed in.

"Tell me about your father," says Doctorpuppet, "tell me all about your father."

Kaz closes up her mouth tight as can be, like an infant refusing a spoonful of cereal. She shakes her head juvenile, she crosses her arms over her chest. But she puts her knee up and extends her other leg. Her body is open and closed all at once to him, inviting and rejecting him. Doctorpuppet is all too familiar with such gestures. He had plenty of patients like her.

"Okay," he says, "we can talk about that later."

I take him back to the moment. I can take him anywhere I like. I take him back to Antonia and the shard of glass and the blazing eyes of the woman he started to love in spite of all the torture and humiliation. I keep him there, suspending time for him. If you have faith in these walls, I am glad, I have mastery of time and tide and custody of Hell. I take him back to alone with nothing but the whispers and the ghosts and the First Girl behind him.

You shut your jowly face. Nobody cares what you like. Doctorpuppet will behave once more.

"Tell me about your father," he insists, I lend some of my strength and make her shake. And she shakes. The upright knee goes down, her arms uncross and she closes her eyes and she opens her mouth. It's obvious what she wants in there.

"He never touched me, but I always wished he would. His eyes were like hands on me and I liked the way they touched me. And I wanted him to touch me. I saw him and my mother together one time. I sat in the doorway and watched until they finished."

Doctorpuppet wants to let her stop but he doesn't. Soon it is no longer me in control but the things that made him mine. Doctorpuppet couldn't be decent if he tried. For some reason he tries to as if he was ever his own. But he is owned by the things that made him mine and he is owned by Kaz's thighs and long, slender toes, and the bit of white belly peeking from under her shirt as she stretches, the sapphire blue of her

24

eyes, the confrontational black of her lipstick. The youth and perfection he missed in Antonia, who I am thinking of letting him use for my amusement.

"Go on," he says, eyes predatory, letting her know that he's examined her up and down. He's palmed the scalpel from his pocket but she doesn't see it.

"I was only little but I knew how to touch myself. I told you I learned how to touch myself early. I developed young in a lot of ways. I think it messed me up. Do you think I'm messed up?"

He laughs. Every time I hear his laugh, it amazes me that none of the others knew better, not the First Girl, who I am shooing, not Antonia, not any of his patients who he had his way with.

"No, I don't think you're messed up. Nobody's perfect, Kaz, we all have traumas and issues and sexual hangups. It's just part of being human. I wouldn't be much of a doctor if I branded you just "messed up," now would I?"

Kaz crosses her arms over her chest, sits up some and smiles.

"I suppose "having one's shit fucked up" isn't in the DSM is it, doc?"

"Afraid not. And if it were, the human race would be on Thorazine."

"I like you," says Kaz, lying back down and stretching more, "you're the best doctor I've worked with."

"I like you too, Kaz," says Doctorpuppet, "and you don't need to worry about infantile sexuality. It's a common thing to be sexually precocious and as a society, we don't really know what to do with it, in the same way that we have trouble dealing with gifted children. Our society might be prejudiced a lot against intellectuals but its prejudices against free sexual expression are a lot worse."

She calculates whether or not she could stretch her foot out into his lap. I convey this information to Doctorpuppet and he leans in. She wants to touch him, therefore he can be touched. She toys with his crotch with her long, bare toes, making it start to quiver and rise. He lets out a moan of contentment.

"I'm not sure we should be doing this," says Doctorpuppet. This is a speech he's mastered many times and has given more than I can count. Doctorpuppet is very good at feigning reluctance and feigning ethics and feigning some measure of decency. There were times in his life when he was good enough to convince himself that he believed that things he was doing were wrong. Those days, of course are gone. And he is infinitely thankful to be free of them.

His fat, vicious harridan cow of a wife is trying to make herself present in the room but I push hard against her. This is not Maddy's time. This is all for Doctorpuppet and all for Kaz. What is that sound? No matter. I'm sure it's nothing. I own all sounds in this place. The tiny clanging could be anything. I shouldn't concern myself over any tiny clanging. Not when something like this is going on.

"How does that feel?" she asks him, foot making intimate circles along his balls. There can be no way she doesn't know how that feels. Not when he stirs underneath her like that, not when she has given herself to the men that she has given herself to. She has come to be absolved of this empty space, this extra cunt inside her that she fills with man after man, she has come to be absolved of this empty space but she has found instead something else to plug it up awhile. There is no stemming the flood, that is for certain.

"Good," he says, with a mock sigh of defeat, a triumph disguised as submission. Nothing worse than a very sore winner. Of course, knowing Doctorpuppet, he's going to pass that soreness on. I will make sure of it. There is a scalpel in his hand after all. As his hardon starts to spring up, she wraps her feet around it and pumps it some.

"Do you want more?" she asks, as if it is a question. She

pulls her shirt over her head, two perfect circles sharpened by his words make their appearance, reinforce the definition of "more" and how much of it there is. She has a sense of what was in this man, so there is no way he wouldn't want more.

"Yes," he breathes, once more in mock defeat. He hangs his head in what is supposed to look like shame. He's getting worse at this part. This is not a man who can even think of, could even imagine what shame looks like now.

She gets off her couch, gets on her knees and crawls.

"Do you have something for me, daddy?" she asks.

"Yes," he says, unzipping his pants. Red and throbbing, foreskin veiny, Clarence presents himself to Kaz, who crawls too fast in her anticipation, spoils the game but fixes it when her lips venture up the organ, then back down. She lets his balls melt into her mouth and begins to suck hard on them. I let him have this completely, remind him why he must be loyal. I let him feel the whole sum of the tenderness and deftness of her sucking him with utter disregard and ignorance of the fact that he is a dead man.

Eyes on his pleading for acceptance from him and everyone else she's done this to and for all at once, her head bobs up and down thirstily accepting and adoring the object of affection and of hunger. He strokes her forehead as she does, keeps eye contact and says just what she wants to hear, what many broken women need to hear.

"Good girl," he says.

Kaz straightens up with pride, fights back tears. He's speaking to her like a dog or a child but it feels so gentle and sincere. She picks up her pace, needs him happy, needs every drop. So empty all the time and nothing fills her. So lonely all the time and nobody's company. Nobody's ever company. But she has this, this thing in her mouth to be good to, this man at the end of this thing to be good to and to be company, to be loving and appreciate and want her to get better. It's a beautiful thing. She picks up her pace, going almost from kind to desperate. Of course there is desperation and seldom kindness. There is so much desperation in these walls, these walls where I am god.

She slowly withdraws him at the first taste of tiny signs of seed. She meets his gaze intensely.

"Should I finish you or do you want something else?"

"I'm not sure this is right, Kaz," says Doctorpuppet, certain this is right, at least for him, that this is wrong, at least for her, that this will be paid for in suffering and shame and maybe eventually blood or almost certainly blood.

"Should we stop?"

"I can't now. We can't now. We have to but we can't. Do you promise you'll forgive me for this? I'm older than you and I should know better. Promise me, promise me, this won't change how we relate."

She pulls down her shorts and her thong.

"I promise."

He gently lays her down on the couch she just crawled off of. The First Girl, the skullfaced composted thing, wants to come out and warn her. I flick the First Girl away like a fly about to land on a bowl of soup. She is faint and distant and weak and broken, tortured beyond the point of ego mostly no good to me but to give someone an occasional spook. Nobody needs to be spooked right now.

He begins by kissing her chest. One long, lingering kiss on the heart. As if to say "this thing matters to me, I will treat it right." His kiss, like any dead man's kiss, is nothing but a lie. She moans out thanks, overplaying it to make him feel like a prodigy at loving. And were he not the keen observer that he is, he would be fooled, no doubt many have been fooled.

He grabs the little chain hanging from her rosy pink nipple which almost fades into the whiteness of her flesh. He plays with it a little, showing a great deal of self restraint.

He wants to yank and shove and rend and tear. He wants to see if he could pull hard enough and the nipple would come off. He died before things like this became popular so never got a chance to play with them so rough. Instead, he kisses her mouth, a kiss that pretends to be somebody else. He is pretending to be a doctor instead of a Doctorpuppet. She sighs into his mouth feeling understood and appreciated and wanted. She is certainly wanted. She is certainly understood. The last one is not something Doctorpuppet ever really did.

He inserts himself. Not gently. No warning. He inserts himself the way he always has, the way he treats people's minds. He invades her and attacks her. But she asked for it and she doesn't seem to mind. It hurts but all she can think is "thank you," all she can feel is that something is in the empty and the empty might go away and there might be no more empty so there might be something else that's not quite empty.

He hammers into her. He ignores the limits of his body, ignores fatigue that he would have later since the body is just on loan, the body will be retracted and he will have all eternity to rest. He pulls his mouth away from hers so that she can scream. And she does. She does scream. I pull it into the walls, I take it in for me when she screams. Someone could be standing at the door and they'd hear nothing.

"Daddy, thank you, daddy…"

He places a hand around her throat. He stops and lets a great gob of saliva drop into her mouth. She coughs some, chokes some as he punishes her for some transgression his older sister made when he was little. He punishes her from the time she put him in a dress or how she'd get naked in front of him and tease him with her body, how she made him masturbate to her when he was old enough to. He punishes her for all those secret shames and all the teasing whores and the bodies before Maddy that she didn't know about and still doesn't. And the one in the woods who came back, the First

Girl. He punishes her for being what she is.

"Thank you, thank you daddy," she struggles out, trying her hardest to keep the beat with a man that just wants to hurt her and does it so very well. He lets loose, not caring that tears are flowing down her cheek and she doesn't want the repercussions of it and doesn't want to walk around full of cum. She doesn't say this and doesn't object because she deserves this and brought it upon herself by being such a worthless dirty whore and for all the shameful secret thoughts she has. She invited him in and invited me in through him. She believed him and developed her faith in these walls.

I take pleasure in knowing the man I can't read has walked into a house of acolytes. This is my temple and Doctorpuppet fills her with apotheosis and faith. So very much faith. He squeezes her throat harder, leans in to bite, does so just hard enough not to make a mark. She can feel the choke and the tooth and the hateful thrust and this is the world to her.

"Do you want to stop?" he says suddenly, adopting the demeanor of a proper doctor, "because if you need to stop, we can. I want you to be comfortable. I want you to be able to trust me."

He pulls out of her and sits, hangs his head down and puts it in his hands.

"This was a mistake, Kaz. I'm so sorry. I don't know what I'm doing. I've hurt you. I never meant for it to go this far. I'm your doctor. You should trust me."

She sits up and rubs his back. She kisses the back of his neck.

"No, you've been good to me, daddy. I need this."

Doctorpuppet shakes his head. He prepares to get his pants back on. Kaz clings to him, wraps her arms around his waist and hangs on tight. She kisses his face and shares her tears with him. Doctorpuppet feels like he might be doing something wrong. Doctorpuppet knows what he's doing.

Doctorpuppet doesn't want to hurt her like this. Doctorpuppet wants to hurt her so much worse.

"I can't…I can't."

He can. He must. He will. He takes her, face suddenly rotting away, revealing the time he has spent in the ground, face suddenly yellowed skeleton with nothing behind his sockets. He grabs her again by the throat, contorts his gumless skeleton mouth into a smile. She stares into the empty holes but somehow is unafraid, somehow knows that it's still him and doesn't care what has become of him, the rot, the gone of him.

"You want me now?"

The scalpel seems to fly into his hand. She chokes and sobs.

"I asked you if you want me now. Do you want me now?"

She strokes his shoulder affectionately. Keeps his gone gaze. Brave girl. Such a brave, demented, stupid girl. She thinks of what he's done for her, thinks of the emptiness and what if he were gone and what if she could never talk to or touch or trust him again and what if it was just her and a world of men who weren't him who wanted only to do her harm instead of fix her. She won't let him be gone. They're always gone. She won't let him be gone.

"Yes, yes I do."

He falls upon her, breathing rot on her face, the stink of time, the reek of loss. She has been brave. I give him back his face and through him, she gets back that very face. The face of this man, of the father she has grown to love and need over the year she's spent here. She would have given herself to him, face or none, or even flesh or none, and she has proven her loyalty.

They move and moan and coil and adore. They roll and rumble and touch each other, absorbed in this moment. The conscience he pretended to have has long come and gone. There are the thoughts cascading through him. Thoughts

31

of knives and hammers and stranglings and keeping her in the cage as he once had Antonia. He wishes he could make them perform on each other and then make them perform on Maddy. He wishes he could once more feel what it is to hold the blade in his hand and make it do its beautiful work.

"What if you can?" I whisper.

"I can't do this to her," he says back in his head, "this is sick. I need to I need to...."

He can't hear his thoughts over the sound of his cock squishing around inside her. He can't hear his thoughts over the need to make use of the object in his hand and make his mark. He needs to make his mark. He needs her so bad in ways that she can't give of her own volition. So I drag him out of her. He sits up straight and stares back at the First Girl, begging him to let her go, telling him she won't tell anybody if he just lets her go, offering herself again if he just lets her go, saying let me go, it will be fine if you just let me go so let me go please please please...

Kaz sits up and once again reaches out for him.

"I told you that it was alright. I told you I didn't care what you were like. I know something's wrong with you but I promise I don't care what you're like as long as you don't leave me here alone. I need you."

He begs me to let him leave now but he doesn't want to. I know what he actually wants and he's going to.

"Lie down," he says.

"Anything," she sighs back, "but please just don't go. I love you. I need you."

Scalpel in hand, he reaches in deep as he can. Scalpel in hand, he drags it along the walls, marking with his print. She screams, she sighs. She huffs and puffs. She bleeds. He pulls it out again, hand covered in blood, scalpel covered in blood, Kaz's insides scraped. Her eyes are wide and tearful. She doesn't understand why he's done this and why it had to happen.

"Thank you," she says, "thank you for loving me."

He strokes her hair, pushes it away from her face and kisses her cheek. He smiles and she smiles back at him, even as some blood pools up on the couch. She doesn't scream. Brave girl. Brave brave girl. She puts her arms around him and drags him close and brings him down. She whispers up into his ears, fugued, says something surprising.

"Cum in me," she says, "fill me."

Her face and body scrunch up from the pain she's in but she accepts him and he complies, no longer begging me, no longer wanting me to let him end her or to free him from this moment. They fuck. And they fuck again. And they roll over and once more fingernails and teeth and passion and hate and wrath, they fuck again. And from his long dead balls full of borrowed life, a gift from the one who is god in these walls, he explodes, filling her with something impossible. Impossible but for the god in these walls. And merciful me, we let her forget the whole thing.

I come to Micah in dreams, in a grove untouched by man, skies obscured by trees as old as time. I am manlike, but as I am better than man, my body is greater. My skin is tan and smooth, my muscles ripple. My head is horned and crowned in leaves, my legs, furry, hooved. My manhood is gigantic, over a foot long, crimson, its head gigantic, the size of a small fist. I stand before him, Pan exaltant. God is talking, he will listen. He bows before me, placing a kiss on the head of my giant cock. He turns around, presenting, offering himself. Micah has become mine.

I get behind him and comply with his will. I force my way into him, bringing the strength of the trees, the strength of the wild into each thrust. I fill him with base nature and brute strength. Blood oozes out but he moans instead of screaming. He is caught up in my musk and in my might. I am feeling something much akin to ecstasy. Joy is not common for me but as I use his inner spaces, we become one, man and Pan.

# PAYING THE PIPER

Bird and rabbit, bear and stag look on.

Deep in the green place that mirrors the Emerald Necklace, he becomes mine completely. Load after load of ectoplasm explodes into his dreamself, into his soul. As he trembles in his sleep, he is cumming and cumming and cumming. Cytherea beside him wakes up, and with a smile takes his dribbling prick in hand and feels his release, the release he's gaining from me.

The ritual rape is now threesome. I, in the world of green, musky, ageless things, her in the bed beside him sharing the pleasure. I do not quite have her yet but I certainly will. I am Pan, the force of his id. I am the voice in the trees that he's been hearing. He spasms and explodes but he stays hard. Godhood in his ass is a powerful force. He is moaning in his sleep, she is drinking sacred nectar, cleaning 'til she decides to bring her roundness down, to take him inside and ride him. She knows by his twitching he is experiencing something magical and she must have it. They think that they believe that love must be free but the both of them are deeply jealous.

She wonders as she lowers herself, envelops his cock, if the dream lover was her. As she bounces, taking it in, she longs to outperform me. His body wants to drag him from the forest to get him back with the cow he's chosen to pair with, fool that he is. His body wants to watch her giant udder bounce up and down as she works him. It wants to take him away from this spiritual communion.

But I am in the primeval spaces where the call of gods and satyrs is loud as can be. Though the cowcunt tries to claim him, he is mostly mine, mine for slippery goatcock, mine to own and mine to use as I desire. And for some reason that I don't understand, I want to know him and take his insides as mine even as I compete with the cow that he professes to love. I understand him inwards now so he'll be more mine than the other's and soon as much mine as he can be. He revels in my pounding, heart and prostate tickled by my affections.

Then I let him halfway into consciousness because I want to see what he'll do. He doesn't disappoint. He gets right to pushing the cow off of him. He gets on top of her, grabs one of her long, hard nipples in each hand as he reenters her with a thrust that is almost combative. She screams and smiles gigantic.

"Fuck me," she moans, "fuck me, you fucking beast." She has no idea how right she is and what she is asking for. His thrusts exit quickly, so he might get back in, hips empowered by the satyr strength. He thrusts hard, the thrusts rapid, he thrusts berserk, cock stampeding into cunt. He is half in, half out the forest and as he fucks her, I am fucking him, unloading over and over again. He is, after all, mine and each spasm reconfirms it, earning it and taking it once more. Smiling and begging for it. The whore is smiling and begging for it. She ignores the pain though the lining of her cunt must be tearing under his strength. He is so asleep and so awake at once.

"Harder!" she screams, "Harder! Fuck me, you beast!"

It is possible she feels that what's in me is in him, me fucking him as I fuck her. Her cunt is strangely tight. It feels good. She is not an awful lay. I can almost see what he sees in her. There is value in her cunt, strength her mind and will are lacking. Her shouldbe gaping pussy is tightening around him, just as his asshole is tightening around the cock of dreams, the cock of Pan triumphant. How dare you make me greedy you filthy vermin, how dare you shits show me how much there is to have and to take.

Maddy appears to me, making suggestions. I do not expect to hear from Maddy and surprise is one of the few sensations I am not acclimated to. Doctorpuppet comes out to watch but his wife is generally bitter, hard and disdainful. Doctorpuppet's soul is slick with shit but Maddy is genuinely made of nothing good. I always appreciated how she was made of nothing good. It is, in this case, quite inspiring. She is pointing to the bottle of wine on the nightstand and it is clear to me immediately what she's suggesting. Maddy does not have good memories of bottles of wine, that's for certain. I will not waste her suggestion. It is inspired.

So Micah picks up the wine bottle.

"Are you going to pour me a drink?" Cytherea asks. He does not answer. Micah is not in a position to speak, even if his life depended on it. His ass is clenched tight, his body filled with the sacred fluids and waves of me. So, no, he most certainly has no intention of pouring her a drink. Instead, he withdraws from her and with a wicked jerk, he replaces his cock with the corked wine bottle, its width and length more than stretching her to her rather impressive limits. She moans.

"Be careful," she says, "this could hurt."

"This could hurt" is hardly among the phrases he could hear or care about at this time. He thrusts without thought, his surrogate glass cock smooth and thick, long and hard. His eyes are distant and wide and gone as gone can be. Maddy looks on, rotund, naked and rotten inside and out. She sticks a pair of thick fingers into her illused tunnel of a vagina, working the shards of her demise around as she stirs the audibly thick, bloodied juice.

She shows herself to Cytherea, a dead woman frigging herself fiercely. Cytherea's eyes widen in fear as her ass widens in pain and pleasure. Cytherea is dilating, her body an eye opening to terror.

"Stop!" she cries out as if this is a word that the puppet of

Pan recognizes, "I saw something! We're not alone!"

Maddy giggles into her right hand as the left one works herself, getting chips of glass into its too thick fingers. She appreciates having been seen. Maddy is not someone who has gotten much of pleasure. She whispers to me about the moment she can't let go of, even as she works her wide, inarticulate cunt, making her rotted, shapeless tits flop up and down. Micah watches her as well, She shows him the moment where she was ended, with blood and great oozing red puddles of her lifeforce. His whorish cow is screaming, wants it in, wants it out.

Still full of lust, he resists Maddy's suggestion to take Cytherea outright and give her to me completely. A part of him loves her and this part surrenders to an atom of judgment. I hope this part of him will not linger long.

He opens up the nightstand and resists me and denies me and lies to himself by withdrawing the bottle of lube he keeps in there, rubbing it into her asshole even as she cries and begs him to answer her, even as she screams about the dead woman furiously fucking herself bloody. Vulgar display. Needs a lesson taught. And here he is using lubrication. I growl at him to fuck her dry but he will not fuck her dry. He doesn't want to hurt her though he wants to hurt her. She certainly deserves it. He could be rid of her and I'd help him but instead he has uncorked the bottle so he might slide it in the hole.

She is crying as he takes her with it, though her lubed asshole absorbs it and brings it in fine, wide and smooth as it is. I drive into him harder as he drives into her, my great phantom cock pounding at such a pace that he blacks out into the jungle into the sensation of being perfectly had. She is screaming now and begging him to stop. Maddy wants him to break it and rip her insides. Yes, that's the way. He can't really hear her though.

Cytherea eventually bites her tongue and rides the

rapewave into new sensation. What a man, what a beast, what a god her lover is. She has asked for the beast and now the beast has come.

Somehow, she has never loved him more. She needs to have him like this, even though it hurts her, stretches her, tests her limits and her faith in him. She wonders what got into him, not knowing that it is me. If it could be, as it will be, I could be all that's in him, the thing that twists her wide open and uses her hard, cum after cum after cum.

Still tearing into her with the bottle, he inserts his cock. She's getting wet and tense and tight. If he could care right now, he'd take pleasure in her pleasure instead of just his and mine. He is taking much pleasure in me, here in the deep green tangled would where he is had and had completely. He starts cumming in her as I cum in him, fluids and fluids and fluids begetting fluids. She is begging him to stop even as she gets pleasured. She keeps swearing that she saw Maddy, which she has, even though she hasn't, even though she has. She has seen the sloshing heavytitted, thumping meatskinned monstrosity, corpseskinned graygreen, empty-eyed harridan.

She screams from pain and ecstasy, she screams for him to stop and to keep going and she screams "not my ass" and "no no no no." Shit and blood and lube are seeping from her gaped asshole. She screams that she is going to die. Micah hears nothing, since he is in the woods, untouchable by anything in the world but me. His cock and the bottle are hurting her.

I show some discipline by opening Micah's eyes to let him see the mess he's made of his woman and her cunt and her ass and her bed. He is out of the jungle. He's mine now but I give him his body and spirit so he can feel what he's done. He doesn't clean up. He doesn't call a doctor. He looks on into the future and at the woman beside him, who he loves or claims to love. She is sobbing, bleeding and cumming, holding a towel up to her ass to stem the bleeding, which should stop. At least he hopes it will and hopes it can stop.

He holds her close, kisses her. Though she is still bleeding, a smile crosses her face.

"I liked that," she says, "so do it more like that."

I move through the fluids inside her, move through her body and blood to patch her up some, to fix her. To make her ready for worse next time.

# BASEMENT

Without the equipment, he's felt insignificant. He barely touches it. The guitar. It reminds him of somebody. He's more into the piano anyhow. He's felt naked without his equipment since he usually isn't much of anyone. He had breakfast with Micah and Cytherea and they were nice enough or acted nice enough but he still feels like he doesn't fit in. He doesn't. Not yet.

He doesn't yet fit in. The conversation had been stunted. He asked if the house made noises. Micah had joked about ghosts. And everybody shared an awkward laugh. He had not felt much like trusting either of them. There is something about them that unsettles him. Micah is a bit too friendly. He talks right in people's faces, frequently touching their arm or shoulder.

Cytherea is aloof when she's not being crude and a bit too forward sexually. She leaned in, giving Brian a view deep down her shirt and joked that the moaning was probably just Kaz with a stripper from the club. Kaz doesn't go to that club actually. Not anymore. Cytherea is mostly just being mean and wants Brian to herself. She thinks it will make Micah jealous. Getting a good fucking and making Micah jealous in one fell swoop seems like a great deal to her. She likes his face and his casual scruff, the little bit of muscle on his body, the broad shoulders. She wants him more than she had the previous day. Of course.

Just for fun, I sent her the image of the two of them fucking. He was behind her as Micah had been, hands twisting her nipples, cock smacking into her overstretched cumtunnel. Made her wet. Gave her ideas that she already had. I think this should be amusing. Micah would never admit he gets as jealous as she does. They are precious and chaff to each other all at the same time. They are expendable things that they could never actually live without.

Kaz had had a morning session with Doctorpuppet. She had once gone to see a doctor outside the house. She didn't need that anymore. It didn't help her anyway. She had once wasted an hour and a half of her week in an office space in Brookline lying about whose hands had been on her body the weekend before, lying about how much she loved and how much she hated herself, lying about all the poisons she put inside to make living tolerable and then lying when she pretended she didn't notice the therapist staring at her chest. When Doctorpuppet does it she likes it.

Doctorpuppet is an interesting case. There is no reason the ladies should have been swooning and sighing and sopping over him and yet they were and yet they are and yet they would do anything for him. She lies upon his couch, the couch in the study and he listens and not once during her account of her week does she lie to him. And all her wrong and ugly and open gash is lain bare for her and him. Doctorpuppet almost forgets himself and his life by having pangs of guilt for wanting to have and to use and to taste her. He wants her to walk away from this and to leave the house, my threshold and to never come back here again. She wants him to be her own to prove that she has broken down his power, to prove that she could break any man down.

Leah is in class. Micah and Cytherea are out. They'd had a big night and feel close. And Kaz is talking to Doctorpuppet. So, Brian is alone down in the basement, setting up his things so he can get productive and feel like his own man and feel like whatever he had to leave behind, the thing I can't look at, is gone and that it is its fault and not his that he had to leave it. I don't understand his allergy to nostalgia. I am not sentimental but I am fond of nostalgia.

He is stacking black boxes and setting up boards covered in knobs. I have some idea what they are because I have seen them in Micah before but as far as I'm concerned they are nothing but strange boards with knobs on them, tools of the cacophonist trade. I do not wish to know more about how all this works and what it means to him but I must because he has crossed this threshold and I am entitled to him.

He plugs in the keyboard, sets up the microphone stand, sets his guitar down in the corner to collect dust. A man so averse to nostalgia no doubt lets a great deal of his life collect dust. Pathetic thing, this man surrounded by machines to reconfigure the noises of his life, the new one in this house, the one he doesn't gather yet. While resistant to inquiry, I'm hoping that he can be educated.

He looks to the guitar and then away from it. He grabs a beer and he sits, contemplating the thing as if he does not even know the function of the device. No. It's not that. It's something better than that. Interesting. He's put the guitar down someplace very special, one might say he has set down at the heart of the basement.

It's my favorite patch of the past that belongs to me and the person in the patch, oh, she's my favorite. I shouldn't have favorites. It's a sign of sentiment. I am not sentimental. I'm above that. Though often I see these people lose things and it occurs to me that it would be quite terrible to lose something or someone. I almost lost the girl who left but she was too much mine. Because of this and because he seems to know I feel like communicating with him some and conveying some of my many stored up moments, since my many stored up moments are so very important to my architecture.

The corner, the precious corner, held Antonia; Antonia, of the dirty blonde hair and eyes that sparkled with enthusiasm even when Clarence brought her home for dinner. They ate coq au vin, cooked oh-so-perfect by quiet, devoted Maddy.

She didn't notice the red wine was making her terribly sleepy. But she noticed when she woke up to Clarence inside her, stoic silent wife looking on as he had his way with her.

"Come fuck her, Maddy, come fuck her," he had said.

"H-h-help…" Antonia struggled out, words speared to death on the edge of her abuser's cock. And Maddy just shook her head at both suggestions. Never liked little whores like this one. I don't show him this because I'm not in deep in yet and he's not ready to know it. The truth will be a whole lot less enticing so I show him the part that entices, I show him the cage. But most importantly and most enticingly, I show him the girl in the cage.

Antonia, both fair and dark of hair is in the cage splayed naked and inviting. She's rubbing her clit while she spreads her lips wide open. He tries to blink and make her go away. He tries to tell himself that there is no cage. She is the scent of pie baking on the wind, the chime of doorbells with the news of longawaited packages from the family. She is for him here and now, though I only give him enough glimpses of her to know he saw it and she was certainly there.

He lets go some and I can get glimpses of him just as he had of her. He thinks something is terribly wrong. Loving cannot be this easy. It's got drama, it's got hurt and there's never a happy ending. Love is to him perhaps like the life of the real Antonia instead of like this vision of her. It wasn't real before. Before what? Intriguing. Love smells like her situation. These thoughts are pregnant with promise, as open as Antonia the dream, Antonia the ghost.

A frame of Maddy is angry. Stay away from that whore! Nobody touches that whore! I push her back, drag her to the time of the broken bottle, when the whore she hated went and Christened her like a ship. Brian doesn't quite see when she shows up but still feels a moment where he is drawn away from lust and into melancholy. I am very angry at Maddy for this. I do not like when she acts like she's not mine. She is

43

mine. I won her fair and square. Antonia and I won her fair and square. Antonia, who I freeze before his eyes to let him linger on the possibilities.

He feels she must be so. He does not know but he sees it and he feels she must be so and therefore must be present. He reaches toward her, not knowing their distance is the distance between life and death, between the present and history. This is a wide chasm. I can't believe when he says it but he does.

"I can see you. It's okay."

"I-I could…" Antonia says to me, "you know, I could…"

I wait for her to say it.

"I could touch him if you want me to. He wants me to. You're making him want me and I can do that for him. He'll let me."

"Don't listen to that dirty little whore," growls Maddy, "you mustn't listen to it!"

"I'm sorry," says Antonia to Maddy, "I didn't mean to."

"That's a lie!"

Antonia hangs her head.

"It is."

Maddy shrieks loud enough that it almost shakes my hold on her and I have to tense up the strings. I grab hard onto her tethers. I do not approve of behavior like this and I have made it known. This is not a place where insubordination is allowed to thrive. If insubordination is allowed to thrive, then I lose hold of what is mine, if I lose hold of what is mine, then then then then then then then I don't know. I don't want to think about it.

"She will kill you 'til you listen, bitch," I growl throughout her essence, "she will fuck your husband right in front of you. She will rip your cunt with broken glass then rip it up again until you listen. You are impertinent sometimes, Maddy. I give you so much and what you do give me? You give me your anger and disdain. I will not take anymore of that."

I consider punishing her but I take her instead to the places where she was putting Antonia in her place, the place where torture and beatings were given out freely and the thing in the cage knew that it was nothing but an object for everyone's pleasure. She would sit beside her in church, her eyes aglow and would regard her as mother. She had almost become a mother.

"I'd like," said Antonia, "to touch him, just once, please let me touch him."

"Just once," I said, "but wait."

"I will be good," replies Antonia, "I am always good."

The First Girl, sobbing cadaver, wants to come out again and sob. But this is not the time. I send her back to her moment, the one where Clarence gave her to me. I am feeling a bit repulsed by the thing, though it is not normally in my nature. She is not completely mine or even completely there. There is so little to do with it. I turn my attention toward Antonia instead.

"You will get to say hello," I tell her, "for I am a loving and giving god."

"I know this," she replies, "you are a god of love and justice and you give me everything I deserve."

It is easy to see why Antonia was Clarence's treasure, the things in her that men would so desperately want. Always willing to learn and always retaining what you teach, such a delight. Her heart and her mind are so open and she wants so very much to be good. It brings me joy, as close to joy as I can get, or it gives me the thing that I think is joy.

"Hello," she whispers to Brian.

He catches it. Was it another noise from the walls? It can't be anything else. He still has to open a third beer to pull himself together. His eyes still keep drifting to the corner of the room though.

# SESSION II

"Maybe you need to stop being passive," says Doctorpuppet to Kaz, "maybe you need to make an effort. You let too many people control you. Phillip, Doreen. You let too many people control the momentum of your life. That's why you keep having dreams of your car skidding off the road. You're skidding off the road. You feel like you're losing control of your life."

"I am," says Kaz, trying not to take a defensive tone, "I went to an audition last week."

"Good. And how did it go?"

"The warm-ups were hard and the other girls...well, holy shit, you should have seen them."

"And you?"

"And me what?"

"How do you feel compared to them? Are you as good as they are? Are you as attractive?"

She laughs. It's a stiff and uncomfortable laugh. It answers the question quite clearly even though she doesn't know it does.

"I'm way hotter than all of those girls. One of them is dating one of my exes. He's totally settling. She's got a face like a fucking horse. I swear to god, like a fucking horse."

"And how were they as dancers?"

She doesn't answer. Which is an answer. But then she answers.

"They're better trained technically. But there's something I have that they lack, some big, wild bestial thing. They're not in touch with their shadows and they don't do enough with their arms and shoulders. They more than kept up on

46

the warm-ups but everything they did was honestly really fucking boring. They were all probably really terrible in bed."

Kaz extends her leg invitingly.

"When it comes right down to it, they're not as pretty and they're not as smart and they're not as interesting as I am."

"Mhmm," says Doctorpuppet. He is quiet for a little, letting his eyes traverse her luscious, impossible calves. Doctorpuppet's begging me to let him touch her again. It would be wrong again to do so. But he doesn't care that it would be wrong to do so though he doesn't care if it would be wrong to do so. He doesn't care even though it sickens him. He would do anything to get back the thing I recently gave him, the moment as flesh, the moment to serve me. He wants to feel the bristles of her Mohawk yet again.

"Do you think it's your hair? Could that be a part of it?"

"Yeah," she says, "that's a part of it. None of them look alternative. None of them are cool, none of them are creative, none of them even really look that hot when they dance. And this is burlesque, so that's kind of the fucking least of it."

He's quiet again, waiting for my answer to his petition. I give him something like a maybe which is actually a no. I want to see him holding onto the possibility as this progresses. I have to promise him something sometimes. Can't be all punishment and yet I cannot spoil them. The silence is still and awkward and that silence is larger than life.

"I don't believe that," says Kaz, "I'm scared that I'm not good enough and that nobody will ever love me. When I look in the mirror, it's never as good as it could be and I'm constantly comparing everyone and it doesn't quite stack up. I'm scared that I can't do this and I'm not good enough and I can't do anything to change that. We go over this a lot and I don't know if I'm getting better or I ever will."

Doctorpuppet reclines in his chair. He does not need to

but the pantomime of life is very important. The first time he came out, she did not believe he was there. The second time she was even more skeptical, afraid that this was a recurring hallucination. But the times she had spent unsatisfied in those overpriced office suites in Brookline made her terribly receptive. She did not want to spend any more time in a cocoon of exploitation and silence and in that silence and exploitation, she heard the voice that told her to go to the study. She suddenly found messages on her phone from his secretary and started confirming appointments. If the messages were on her phone, they were real. She saw them there and heard the secretary's voice. She is certain now that he's present. Which he is. It's simply that he's not alive.

"Have you heard the serenity prayer? The serenity to accept the things you cannot change, the courage to change the ones you can and the wisdom to know the difference?"

She perks up slightly.

"Yeah, of course."

"Well, what can you change?"

"I want to stop feeling isolated. Leah's boring, Cytherea's a bitch and Micah's a space cadet. I don't feel like I have much of anyone to talk to but you. I have friends but they're always really busy. I don't know what the fuck's up with my friends."

"What about the new guy?"

"He seems to need a lot of alone time. Musicians are like that. They need all this time to themselves to practice and record and shit and to get used to the place."

Doctorpuppet nods clinically, mechanically.

"Well, can you help him get used to the place?"

"I can, I guess. But I'm afraid."

"What are you afraid of, Kaz?"

"I'm afraid that it will be like it was with Julie again. We didn't always get along. We got along okay most of the time. She was a good buffer too. But we didn't always get along. But now she's...you know. And I miss her. What if that happens again?"

She begins to sob. In life, he would have had to make some move to comfort her because that would have been his job. But here? But now? His job is nothing but to make her mine forever.

"Are you saying that it was your closeness to Julie that drove her to kill herself, like being close to you drove Phillip away and made Doreen hurt you?"

"I don't know if I'd go quite that far," she said, still stifling sobs, "but I'm afraid of it. I can't get close to somebody else. They'll hurt me. They'll use me. They'll leave. That's what people do. Maybe they don't sometimes but I don't know if I want to chance it again. I can't stand that happening."

Doctorpuppet chews his pen cap. It's a nice touch. He asks me again to let me touch her. This would be the perfect time. He knows what he's talking about. He's a psychologist, he knows people's minds and behaviors. And he is right. But I am silent. But I know human nature just as well and I know not to give him what he wants when he is not giving what I want.

"I think there's a difference between getting into a relationship and showing common courtesy to somebody who just moved into your home. I think that isn't something you need to worry about. I think you'll be happier if you bother to reach out to the people who live in your home and get to know them and become part of their lives. If you can't do that in your own house, then reaching out to others is going to be come really tough and you're gonna keep feeling stuck and alone and unable to connect with people around you."

"I guess you're right," says Kaz, grabbing a tissue, "this is the space I live in and I need to relate to it right."

"I think that's going to help you," says Doctorpuppet.

"I think so too," says Kaz.

And so the wheels are in motion. The session ends and she goes and fixes her makeup. Then fixes it up again. Her relationship with her face is ambivalent at best. She goes and listens at the basement door for the sound of singing or instruments or the telltale click of recording equipment. Hearing nothing and nobody, she descends the stairs. She is hesitant at first because she saw something once there that she didn't like very much. She sometimes suspects that basement might be haunted.

She finds Brian down there drinking a beer and staring at the corner of the room where she had seen that thing that one time. Her viscera knots and tells her that it looks like he too has seen that thing that she saw the one time and doesn't want to believe she saw, the girl with the not-quite-there face, reaching out as if to warn her about something, something that she would not listen to warnings about even if they were strongly presented by vehement dead girls in basements. In spite of this, she sits down beside him.

"Hey," he replies. I let Antonia flicker in and out of his vision.

"How's the move been?" Kaz asks.

"It's been good," he answers, as if there's something else that would possibly be okay for him to answer.

"That's good," says Kaz because if his move had been good, it would be good. And just good. Kaz sideeyes the stairs, contemplating the thought of running back up them. The quiet is tense, pregnant with little sounds none of which are at all pleasant.

"Would you like a beer?" he asks. Kaz isn't certain she'd like a beer. But she doesn't want Doctorpuppet to think she's bad and not making an effort to get to know the people around her. If Doctorpuppet thought she was bad, she'd die, she'd absolutely die. And maybe she would actually like a beer and Brian seems nice enough. Attractive in his way. They haven't spent much time together yet so she can't quite judge.

"Yeah," she says, " a beer would be nice."

Because a beer might actually be nice. There is nothing in the corner of the room right now. There was never anything in the corner of the room. They are alone and unburdened. She opens a beer and they go back to sitting quietly and tensely.

"I like it here," says Brian, telling a half truth. If by here, he means the basement full of Antonia, gaping and welcoming, hungry, adoring Antonia, narrow-hipped, dirty, nasty, innocent Antonia. Yes, he likes the thought of his cock in her so he likes it down here.

"Yeah," says Kaz, slicing the half truth in half again, "I like it here too."

Brian sees the quartered truth right away.

"But?"

"But what?" says Kaz, taking a giant gulp of her beer, "there's no but."

"Sorry," says Brian, "thought I might have heard a but in there."

"You didn't. I like it here. Does it seem like I don't?"

She glares at him, nervous and inquisitorial all at once, calling her questioner a cannibal as she wipes specks of flesh away from her mouth.

"No," says Brian, "I'm sure you like it here just fine."

They quietly finish their beers. They quietly grab another beer apiece. I send vibrations through the pink carpet, letting them sit on undulating waves of skin. The hair on both their arms stands up and each of them has to stifle a sigh or maybe even some less dignified noise.

"But even with four other people," says Kaz, "sometimes I get very lonely here. This is a quieter house than it seems like. It gets so quiet sometimes that you hear these noises."

"Lonely?" asks Brian, as much a statement as an inquiry. He doesn't want to think about the last part of her statement, I think. There is something about the thought of these little noises that makes him extremely uncomfortable.

"You know I like everyone, right?" she asks, half lying.

"Yeah."

"But they're not all the way there. It's like someone scooped something out. I don't think they're bad people but you know what I mean."

"Yeah."

The two can only carry the burden of so much talk and self reflection. Kaz's shoulders, toned as they are by dance, still can't hold much weight. They go back to drinking beers again. They drain them halfway and suddenly they're just sitting, sitting on the suddenly pulsing skin carpet. Antonia thinks of a song. A song about the sea of love and she hums it and the hum reverberates through the room and it shakes hearts and ears and minds with it. Antonia is slightly out of tune but Antonia is always slightly out of tune.

"Leah is nice," says Kaz, "but she's busy and she's shy and she's a bit stuck up. Not like arrogant but proper. She's really proper. She's disciplined too and I mean, I respect that but it makes her a hard person to know. I don't think I really know her, you know?"

"She's nice," says Brian, "we hang out some."

Kaz itches her arm. She suddenly feels awkward and jealous. She doesn't want to think of him maybe liking Leah. Proper, skinny and disciplined Leah. She did ballet. Kaz's parents had said ballet was bourgeois. Kaz didn't care what was bourgeois. She would never get to be so graceful as perfectly skinny balletic Leah, the perfect China doll medical student of every parent's dreams. The rolling fingers of pink carpet calm her down some, agitate her some. And now she is just feeling desperate.

"That's cool," she says, this time lying all the way.

"Yeah. I like her."

"Cool."

The second beers empty out. Therefore, third beers are

opened. They are starting to get very relaxed, Brian palpably drunk from the drinking that happened earlier and Kaz very buzzed. She is moving closer to him nudged beneath by the fibers of invisible carpethands. Yes, that's the excuse. It's always best to have a proper excuse for these things.

"And Micah and Cytherea are so caught up in their relationship, their relationships. And you can't help but feel like they're not getting what they need from each other and like they're just into some shit that they can't stop."

Brian shrugs.

"I haven't gotten to hang with them much. Micah seems cool though."

"Yeah."

"But everyone's always wrapped up in their own shit. "

"Yeah, guess everyone's like that. That's why it's called your shit, you know? 'Cause it's like you're shit."

Kaz knows she has said nothing profound. Kaz knows she is just barely speaking. She nonetheless feels like maybe this man has granted her some perspective. Maybe in a way this is true and that she is not too far gone to get some but I of course hope this isn't so because it is in my best interest that she stay as she is. She has crossed my threshold and she is rightfully mine.

"They're all so distracted."

"Everybody's distracted," says Brian, who is very, very drunk.

Kaz gets up into a kneel, sitting on her feet and rocking and looking him straight in the eye. Her eyes are gleaming crystal, eternal ice. Her eyes are binding and when they meet his, they become the law. He can't even look away into the corner where he saw what he saw and she had seen what she had seen.

"Maybe," she purrs and slurs, "we can use a distraction."

"What kind of distraction?" he asks, knowing full well what kind of distraction.

"The good kind."

She kisses him. He is too drunk to stop and think but even sober there is no way he would stop and think. He kisses her in return, the two kisses enmeshing into something else. And hands begin to seek out knowledge of bodies. His hands are soon on Kaz's breasts and hers are soon on his crotch. Their kisses get needy and desperate and practically sad and their groping, awkward, drunk and intense. They have soon pulled off each other's shirts.

They follow the rhythm of the hum in the carpet until she overtakes him, pushing him down less than gently, letting his bared back feel the sighs and shudders and touch of the living pink carpet. She guides his hands back to her breast and the piercings in her nipples that Doctorpuppet wanted to use so ill.

"Pull," she whispers, "pull."

He does not need to be told twice to pull. The intent of the piercing is extremely clear. He takes hold of them and guides her body as she moves around on top of him, springing him up to excitement. She releases him, starting to suck. He forcibly spins her body around, pulls her shorts down, leaving her undressed completely. He pulls her down onto his face to taste her deeply. Their bodies linked, they drink of each other.

As the living take pleasure, the dead look on. Antonia is pleased to have inspired such an act. She knows how much it pleases me and it always pleases her to please me. Maddy looks on judgmentally. Doctorpuppet looks on in envy. The First Girl looks on confused and melancholy, barely there at all.

Brian loops two of his fingers into the piercings again, putting pressure on them and pulling her nipples into greater hardness. He uses another finger to stroke her asshole until it begins to relax and he can thrust it in deeper, leaving all three of her holes sealed by hand, by his cock and by his tongue.

She cannot help but pull away from his face and take him into her sex. Antonia's humming and the humming of the rug vibrate in her.

She turns back around. In spite of all the pleasure, she still wants to make sure she has momentum and authority. She finds it hard to trust, even in this context. While he might be pulling on and torturing her breasts, she is still the one on top and still the one who must be in control of the situation. She is the one exaltant, she is the one who can feel some of the power returning to her, some of the beauty and the confidence taken from her by the women at the audition, taken from her by the ever skinny Leah.

"I think I hate her less," Maddy whispers to me, "I think I understand."

"You like that? Hmm?" Kaz shouts, suddenly possessed by the confidence, strength, momentum and control of the situation.

"Yes," Brian moans, "yes."

And he clearly does but suddenly feels a surge of lust, suddenly feels the intensity pouring into his back and the emotions the basement has soaked up, the emotions that this place is now made of. He sits up abruptly sheathing himself in her. Then, using the newfound control, to push her off of him onto her back. Now she is one with the carpetsighs and he is the one surging with most of the power and confidence. He grabs her long legs, spreading them apart as far as they spread and reenters her. Manhood deep as it can get, he thunders into her as Micah was thundering into Cytherea, as a man touched also by Pan, lust, murder and history.

She is screaming and she is not sure if she is begging him to stop or go faster, stop or go faster, stop or go faster. There is almost no way that she could decide. She wants this. She didn't know she wanted this but she wants it. There's a reason she came down here. It wasn't just to please Doctorpuppet. Doctorpuppet, salivating, jealous, is not all that pleased.

Garrett Cook

"You may touch him once," I whisper to Antonia, who drifts toward him. And she touches him just once, her fingers whispering a faint "hello" through his unkempt hair. And deep inside this woman he barely knows, in a basement where he feels murder, lust and confusion, he lets go and fills her with himself. He still keeps thrusting willing himself and working himself hard as he can. And then it happens once again, he fills her and then does it a third time until he must roll off of her, spent and beaten.

But there is wrath and determination still in Kaz's eyes. There is desperation also in her heart. She wants him to remember her right now, powerful, lovely and unyielding. She reaches for his flaccid cock, takes it in her hand and begins to stroke, kiss and suck it back to its former size and might. He wants to voice his objection and say "no more" but he is drunk, entranced and full of passion for her. He says nothing as she gets him hard again and then says nothing as she gets on top again.

She is vengeful in her techniques, sadistic and almost cruel. I start to move in her some, as much as Brian beneath her is starting to move. She let me touch her through Doctorpuppet after all. Brian is struggling and surrendering all at once. He places hands upon her sides to guide her in her affections. She mostly follows his directions though, mostly complies. She holds back her orgasm, thinking of the girls that she thought were better than her and of all that she was jealous of. How easily this act becomes an act of conquest, the opening salvos in a battle with a clear winner and a much too clear loser.

Brian would stop if he could. He is half conscious. He is more than half drunk still. She feels somewhat right although she does not feel quite right because she isn't. But that dread only serves to inspire a deeper, more meaningful surrender. He does not resist the dread but he lets it stir his body and fuel him with adrenaline to use for the conflict at hand.

He pushes up and down with her, makes him take her deep and then practically tosses her off of him. So she gets the full measure, the full slide in and out and she begins to shake. Though Kaz is the one on top, the one desperate to resume the struggle. She trembles and lets out a moan, not the theatrical things at the start of the dance but something true, something with heart and guts and cunt in it. In this battle resumed, she has drawn first blood.

She continues as long as she can, not content until she has gained as much of his fluid as she can and it isn't very long before he once again "rewards" her. And he rolls over, exhausted and confused and beaten once more. She dismounts and without a word, she gathers her clothes, which is just well because there is nothing he has to say to her. There was certainly excitement. She is certainly one of the sexiest women he's seen, you can see that in him. But he must see that there's something that's very much not right about her. Does it have something to do with the cage in the corner where the girl was splayed? What hope does any man have when the girl of his dreams is splayed open waiting in a cage in the corner of the basement?

He has touched me some so I can get into him a bit. He feels guilty. He doesn't know why this happened although he is of course quite sure. Sure as a man who sees does things that he is sure he shouldn't.

"I don't think we should do this again," he says, although he obviously wants to in spite of how wrong it feels. And it feels very wrong.

Kaz looks at him, eyes wide but not at all receptive. Someplace very distant.

"Shouldn't what?"

Brian says nothing, sensing she genuinely means it.

# ABSENT FRIENDS

The girl who left sits with Leah on her bed. They have said nothing to each other. Leah is fairly sure she is seeing things. It is a little late for the onset of schizophrenia, she reasons but that doesn't mean that it can be ruled out. She has experienced voices and racing thoughts as of late and these are not things that are the product of a sane mind, the crystalline mind of a doctor. She will never be a doctor.

"I think you should go," she says to her friend, timid but resolute, certain of what she wants.

"I have," Julie says.

"Then I think you should stay."

And she does but now there is silence. Leah closes her eyes and counts to ten like she did when she was a child afraid of monsters. Monsters and ghosts are flimsy unreal things and they would surely vanish if she took the time to concentrate and think and count to ten. Julie doesn't vanish. Julie exists. Contrary to certain things that Leah knows to be facts, Leah counts to ten and yet Julie is still there. In spite of what she knows about the nature of life and death, Julie still persists.

Leah is trying hard not to ask what it was like. It's the sort of thing that a doctor ought to know if they have the chance to know it and it should be impossible for her to know it so she didn't think that she would have the chance. But at the same time, it seems like something that simply can't be asked. It must be terribly rude so she doesn't. She decides that if her friend is here then her friend is here, even if she isn't. So she sits with her and she starts to feel a bit better. She starts to feel a lot less lonely too. She could go see Brian in the basement but the households in the house are clearly delineated and privacy is important. Leah is a household. Nobody wants to see Leah.

"How are your studies?" asks Julie. Julie doesn't find this interesting or particularly pertinent and Leah talked way too much about her studies. This is hard on Julie, who serves as a lesson about leaving and how it mustn't be done.

"It's good. It's tough. It was hard for a few months, since you…" Leah stops herself, mouth agape, she puts a hand over it, stuffing the words down, one of few things she's stuffed down lately. The fruit, even the fruit starts to rot. None of it is for eating. She doesn't know just how much it hurts Julie. It's not as if Julie can think of very much else beyond this.

"I'm doing better again though. I feel better than I did."

Julie wants to hug her friend but is afraid that would betray her nature. Which it would. I will not permit her to touch and I can't let her do it for long. And I will not give her this.

"I'm glad you're doing better."

The next words, she struggles with, the next words, she's full of terror about. She refuses. She refuses with all her heart and soul and she simply will not have it since it's wrong. It is hurtful. It is sick. It is wrong of her to say it. She is adamant about not saying it until I take her back to the oven and the moment of escape. She had thought she had found her way out of life and in fact had only found her way into my hands to become mine forever. And as she is mine, I reveal to her that I will tolerate no signs of insubordination.

"You're looking good," says Julie, wracked with pain and guilt and knowledge of that which she's about to bring on, which is something that to her is unconscionable.

"You're filling out."

"Thanks."

She doesn't mean it. Time passes and she is naked again in front of the mirror. She is drawing dotted lines around her breasts.

# RIVAL

There is a song that echoes through the closet. It is no skeletal clanking or settling of walls or rumbling of stomachs, no. There is suddenly a song that echoes from the closet specifically addressed to those like Kaz, who feel the squirm of mystery and shame. There is a song that echoes from the closet and it's asking her "do you know from whence it came?"

There is a song that echoes through the closet that tells her that there is something big inside her. It apprises her of her situation and then it makes a suggestion. And I do not know if I want her to conform to it. It tells her what she needs and she grabs the object in question. She examines the wire hanger and heaves a sigh of relief.

Do I want to let her conform to it? This is a question well worth asking. I do not know if I trust the new noise that has manifested or if she will be better off doing as it tells her. Do I want her to or don't I? The question is an openended one. I don't know the answer. I can almost see the feature, just the gears, just the squeaky ones, the ones that need replacing, the one that give the entire machine its meaning. This act could be the one that gets her fully. Am I confused? Overwhelmed? Is something overwhelming me? There is a song that echoes that echoes through the closet, presenting an unmaking or a making.

The Closetsong's a merry one. I want to comply and have it done. Come on now, whore. Open up the closet. Open it up, whore. Open that door. You'll have to sooner or later. She's sitting on the bed, head between her knees. She's crying and she's scared and she has nowhere to turn.

"Dr. Hoyt."

"Clarence," she calls out, "I wish you were here."

He does too but he knows this is not the time for him and he'd better comply or he'll end someplace very very bad.

"Open the door," the Closetsong hisses, "open the door and fix it, bend it, shape it, wield it as the righteous weapon that it is. You can be free of this. You don't even know if it's his…"

"Who is "he"?" she asks the closet.

The closet doesn't reply, except with a strange shaking. The engine I've built has grown so perfect that it is moving now of its own accord. How delightful. No, I am not frightened. Don't suggest it. I am ambivalent perhaps. I am unsure whether I like this outburst of autonomy if that is what this is. I have a complicated relationship with autonomy.

"Get rid of it," says the Closetsong, "open the door, pull out the hanger, fold it over and get rid of it!"

She leaves the house. She flees the house actually. I don't know where she goes yet. She is gone for hours and it makes me furious. I am not sure if the Closetsong and I are at cross purposes but it is quite possible we are and that maybe it is not that I have made something so perfect that is acting autonomously but that something entered my abode without my notice.

I reach out to the Closetsong to ask what it is and what it has done. But there is no response. It's as if, like Kaz, I have been hallucinating. My comprehension is infallible. All things in these walls or in the minds of those that live between them can be touched by me. It simply is.

"Make yourself known," I say to the closet and the closet says nothing. I wish I had hands that were my hands and my hands alone that could know the sensation of wood that buckles or splinters when I strike it. I would smash it with all the force behind those hands that were just my hands. I could grab a pair of hands to do it for me but I would want to know for myself just how it feels. I need some satisfaction. I could make Cytherea jealous or encourage Leah to throw up but I want a tantrum, something fierce and juvenile.

I don't get the opportunity so the Closetsong is making me very mad and I can't stand it. What do I do when I can't stand things? It's a difficult question for one that always gets what they want eventually. I experience something cold and empty. I don't feel it but I experience it. I am beastly still, looking at the posters on Kaz's walls that mean very little to me even with what I have soaked up from her. I experience her experience of Amanda Palmer or whatever an Amanda Palmer is.

"Whatever you are," I say to the Closetsong, "I will conquer you and in my hands you will hurt. You don't belong here. You intrude in my house."

And of course it gives no answer. I wander into Micah, who is working a punching bag. This is nice, the feel of fist, the crunch, the anticipation of greater power, a closeness to the strength of oaks and the unbridled ferocity of Pan. He's thinking of a woman at the gym. Her skin is a chocolate brown and on her bare shoulder is a tattoo of a Gua from the I Ching. He couldn't remember what it meant so of course he looked it up so that tomorrow he can tell her and compliment her on it.

The boundaries of exuberance and violence get so thin. He is always the brute exaltant. I am spending time getting to know the limbs of the brute exaltant. He seldom thinks of Cytherea, though when he does, she explodes inside his mind to the size of the sun. Seems about right. He imagines life without her and it changes how he works the bag. I've prodded him with the suggestion, a prick to see if he bleeds.

He gushes. His punches become less and less focused. His heart races. He takes a big swig of water and he thinks of stopping altogether but he doesn't. Full of inarticulate fear and a creeping not alone, he pounds on the bag. The punches and the passions of desperate men feel different. This is good. I caution myself against desperation. I am angry to be drawn into such pettiness. I feel suddenly as if they have done wrong introducing this suggestion and I might have sabotaged an experience I need. I am again experiencing frustration, I am again experiencing stupid and numbness.

I break away. I float. Simply me. Simply my doings. I float. And I wait. I have eternity but each moment that I have to wait for what I want something stings me. This could maybe lead to building imperfect structures and imperfect engines. This might have been how the Closetsong got in or even what the Closetsong is.

I go back to Micah taking Cytherea with the bottle, Julie encouraging Leah not to eat. Then Kaz is suddenly taking out the hanger to free herself from the thing that grows in her. Micah is standing over his girlfriend dead from anal bleeding and in a moment of weakness, I whisper, in this moment of weakness I broke it and Kaz is dead and Leah is dead too soon, too soon and gone from here, not mine not mine at all and...I see. Presumptuous thing. I don't know what you are trying to deceive me like this and pull me away but you are my rival and I will punish you.

Kaz gets home alongside a man, in a battered coat, stained shirt, backwards ballcap, his mouth missing a great many teeth. There is a none too subtle reek of slumlife on him. This man is scum. I don't know why she brought him. I didn't ask her to. She leads him up to her room and they're both laughing. Brian has opened his door a crack and looks out. He's disappointed. Their days together must have left a mark but she doesn't even remember it.

His anguish makes me very, very happy. I'm perking up in spite of the random elements and the sudden appearance of this bizarre intruder. I feel perhaps that these random elements might not make me mad for once. I follow her up into her room so that I can see what is being done.

She sits down on her bed and motions him over. She

need not ask him twice. She looks like she does after all.

"Come closer," she whispers, getting up on her hands and knees. He must come closer. There can be no other choice. For some reason, I grasp Antonia, grasp her tight, pull her spirit out from waiting, draw it close to me. I trap her in the moment and I look her over. I am feeling almost nostalgic. I am feeling happy to have every inch of her, wanting her almost as the man with the missing teeth wants Kaz. She is mine but I have to see it. She is mine but I have to actively take her from the toy box, make her dance before my eyes as the seduction continues. This sentimentality is going to make me weak. It is base and I resent it.

He comes closer, he leans in to kiss her and she smashes her forehead against his not hard but just hard enough to surprise him and confuse him. She leans in, kisses him on the cheek and giggles. She licks him on the nose, then playfully bites his cheek and then again, but this time, she does it in a manner that is not at all playful.

"Ow!" he says, recoiling, holding his cheek, "what did you do that for?"

"Why did I do what?" she asks.

"You bit me."

She lies on her back and puts her legs up in the air, still giggling. She rubs the side of his face with her foot, then gives him a light kick and begins to laugh, louder still. He should be scared of her but her beauty keeps his where he is, makes him linger. This is why I find it best to control and appropriate beauty when I encounter it.

He should flee but instead he chooses to stay and pay the price. Do I want him to stay and pay the price? Do I want him at all? I don't know if I'd have anything more than an empty shell like the First Girl if he did. I need surrender and murder isn't quite surrender. I want him though he has very little value. He is still something inside my home. I have no choice but to have him. I am sick sick sick.

"Why did you do that?" he asks her again and the house almost trembles with my laughter.

She looks up at him again, confused.

"Why did I do what?" she asks, "I'm afraid I don't understand you."

"You bit me."

Her finger touches her lip and she squints hard. She is looking for the moment but does not find it though she is cognizant that the moment has fled from her.

"Yes," she decides after finally deliberating, "that sounds like something I would do."

The man starts to back away but he makes no motion to get up and leave. There is no way that he could. Kaz takes her shirt off and his eyes and his cock couldn't find the door if they tried. She looks at him, bare-chested, sincere.

"You came here to fuck me, didn't you? I hope you came here to fuck me."

He nods and crawls closer. She puts her hand behind his head and feeds him a breast, which he takes in with the eagerness one would expect from his position. Her hand returns to his cock as he sucks on her. She pumps it up and down until it's full and confident and while he wants to back off her breast and gets down to business, she shakes her head "no."

"Not yet. You haven't had enough, baby."

She slows down her masturbating so he can enjoy the breast in his mouth and so she can enjoy him enjoying it. His mouth and attention become completely absorbed in the object, the beautiful perfect nurturing object he's devouring. She kisses him gently on the head where she had bumped it, strokes his hair, loosening her grip. The fear in him is just the tiny adrenal surge, the sensation of feelings you can't back away from or don't desire to and he is right to have this feeling of no escape. I am listening to the closet for its insights or its rebuttals but it has none. Is it just sleeping or is it trying to piss me off? I cannot suspect that it would do something as innocuous as sleeping.

She pulls her breast away and playfully slaps him again.

"So did you come here to fuck? Huh?"

He says nothing but his eyes make it clear that he did. She lies down and spreads herself open, expectant. He is hesitant, unsure if this is a trick or if she'll hurt him again. But that doesn't stop him for long. He gets on top of her and starts pounding away like the eager dog he is. She stops him, locking eyes.

"Slow down," she says, "we have all night."

He is surprised by this, as are she and I. He moves away from desperation and into pleasure. Into intent. Their lovemaking becomes different. Slow and tender and probably wrong for strangers. But they take pleasure, smile, moan and feel genuinely connected. This connection is way more desperate than maniacal fucking and the overcompensatory violence aimed at loneliness itself. I even start to pity them. She'll be better off completely mine, away from behaviors like this and the needs that spark them.

But they are happy. It is madness. It is stupid and wrong but they are happy. Why do you do this closet? I must splinter your doors and look inside and move among the dresses. I will find you and I will make you silent. Not silent like they are, not shuddering and delighted.

I search through Antonia and Doctorpuppet, opening up their soulguts to see if there is something amidst the entrails of their memories that can more deeply divine the meaning of this moment and what this thing that thinks I learn would possibly want to teach me. They experience this and each other until it ends, like every connection between two people ends. They finish. And it's abrupt and cruel when they finish.

She begins to cry. He moves to her, puts his hand on her shoulder. She recoils, wrapping her arms around her knees, hiding her face.

"Why did you do it?"

He looks up, dumbfounded of course. As well he should be. They had been having a nice time. Her makeup is running, her eyes are red as she glares at him, pure brimstone.

"Why did you put it in me? How could you have done this? I trusted you."

He didn't know her from Eve not three hours ago. He has no idea at all what she's talking about. I like this. Another pleasant surprise.

She pounces on him, grabbing his throat. She snarls. I thought I had her and knew her so well inside and this should be disconcerting but is instead exhilarating. He struggles, surprised by her strength, surprised by the teeth she is sinking into his face.

Maddy flickers into view at the foot of the bed watching, this man, teeth ripping his face, hands on his throat, sees her, dead, naked and working the glass into herself. He tries to scream.

It occurs to me that I don't want him and that I didn't plan this. It occurs to me this is insubordination and I cannot tolerate that. I struggle my way past the hot, scarlet veil in front of Kaz's eyes. And again, I reach her. She lets go, teeth and hands, horror on her smudged face.

The man runs, out the door and probably down the street, frightened enough that there is probably no way that he will consult the police, even while there was a strip of flesh missing from his face. He will run home, to the solace of his drugs and tell himself that what happened hadn't happened at all.

Kaz is alone with her vodka. She reads the label again and again as if it will change to something else. It doesn't. Kaz is alone with her vodka. I could take her, break her, use her, end her but I don't feel like it. She feels like she is losing control and I feel much the same. I almost want to feel her feeling the vodka because I can't feel it myself. She thinks back to when she wanted to write books. She'd always loved books. Cervantes, Goethe, Shakespeare, Tolstoy. She had wanted to write novels but she'd wanted attention more and her parents told her she was pretty and never that she was smart, never.

Maybe she could still write books. Maybe there is enough of her left. She cannot find enough of herself in herself to answer this question. This is as good a reason as any to not be fond of alone. She always has me because I always have her. I must stop myself from being too proud of her as a possession, though one not quite in my hands yet. I will get indolent and greedy.

Leah is eating buttons. She has recently started eating buttons. She hasn't choked yet but it seems inevitable to her that she will. But she can't resist doing it. Food is unappealing, her body a fat, disgusting blob and all she wants to fill it with is buttons. She lifts up her shirt and takes comfort from the dotted lines she has drawn. The dotted lines are enough for now, the sentiment is enough for now. It won't be forever. I hope the Closetsong won't make her do it prematurely.

She hears a knock on the door, hides the buttons and slowly, tentatively she approaches and opens the door a crack, finding Kaz in the hallway, holding a bottle of vodka.

"I wanted to know if you'd like a drink. I forgot whether you drink or not. But I thought maybe I'd offer you one."

Leah can see there is something very wrong with Kaz. There is always something very wrong with Kaz but she could have sworn she heard someone fleeing the house in a fit too.

"That sounds good," says Leah, "I need a break. From studying. Maybe to just not study anymore tonight."

Kaz sits down upon the bed, wonders why it is that it seems like Leah's swimming in her sweatshirt and why the sleeves are wet with drool. She decides that is better not to bother asking. Leah is under a lot of stress, Leah might be fucked up somehow. She's not going to judge her, not after what just happened. With what just happened, it seems like it would be awfully hard to find somebody who she could dare to judge.

Kaz feels something squirming in her stomach. From somewhere behind my precious walls, the Closetsong asks her to borrow a coathanger. I veto this request. Sneaky bitch of a thing. It will not do. Kaz ignores it and pours a shot of vodka. The time has not yet come to stop ignoring this. But she does stop herself.

"Should we get some juice? Something as a mixer?"

Leah shakes her head.

"No. Too much sugar. We'll drink it straight."

"Yeah," says Kaz, "good point. Wouldn't want any of those empty calories."

She rubs what she believes to be an enlarged belly. Leah does not get the meaning of it. Of course, were she with child, it would be best for her to avoid going out and getting fucked by drug addicts or drinking straight vodka but this is much more complicated than simple live birth. This is a dead man's child. This is alchemy, beautiful alchemy. She pours a shot for herself.

"Cheers."

"Cheers."

The two young women throw back their shot and they sit in the silence that exists between them. This is a forest of silence full of problems and beasts and things unsaid and unspeakable. This silence is a place where nothing can be known. There is so much these two women should know and so many ways they could support each other. They think they are completely different and that these differences cannot be reconciled. Each thinks the other hates them. Each would wear the other's skin and each would know the joys of touching it. But instead they sit here in this silence. I worry that the closeness between people can take them away from me. I have never seen this happen but I see them slip away sometimes. In this silence, there does not seem to be danger of this.

"Brian sure spends a lot of time in that basement," says Kaz.

"I like Brian," says Leah.

"Yeah."

"I'm not sure he's one of us."

"Yeah."

Kaz pours another shot.

"I'm not sure we're one of us."

Leah downs it. Laughs.

"We're not."

Kaz pours herself one. Downs it. Laughs.

"Then who is?"

"Micah. Cytherea."

"Are they the only people here then?"

Leah feels inclined to open up the button jar. Or to add Julie to the list. Julie is one of them, them being everyone. But Julie is dead and Leah is losing her mind and eating buttons and talking to dead girls and drawing circles on her chest, her big, ugly heaving chest. She's not getting fatter at least. At least there's that. But she wants to open up the button jar and sit and talk with Julie. Or invite Julie to talk tonight.

"Maybe they don't have to be. They're kind of assholes," says Kaz.

"I feel like there's something to lose, you know?"

Kaz nods.

"Yeah."

"We should invite Brian up."

They knock on Brian's door. Brian emerges right away.

"Yeah?"

"We're drinking vodka," says Leah.

"I'll drink vodka."

# SHE WILL NEVER BE A DOCTOR

When the vodka is gone, Leah sits alone. She is wobbling, stumbling, about to simply faint. Her body is begging her for food, begging her to just eat a piece of fruit or some meat. Her body wants some sign that she wants it to live. She gives it none. She takes off the sweatshirt and traces the markered lines with her finger and she smiles. She's relieved. The two big bags of fat aren't gospel. This is not her body. This doesn't have to be her body.

It takes some effort for her to grab a handful of fat from her belly since there is almost none. But almost none is still not none. The banana smells like rotten hamburger. And rotten meat is practically excrement. Will she shovel shit into herself to cover her body in more shit, more chaff and garbage? There's simply too much of Leah. The two big lumps are signs that she cannot hide forever in her giant bulky sweatshirts. She'll still know what's underneath.

She opens up her drawer. Takes out the scalpel first, making a short feathery tickle along the place where she'd just run her hand. Come on now, you can do this. You can commit. Let me just get rid of this. Let me please get rid of this, let me just be small and thin and perfect enough, let me just be quiet and tiny enough to hide. But she doesn't. She puts it down. Puts it back in the drawer and reaches for something else.

She's been chewing hair and nails but that's not enough. There needs to be something that isn't part of her. Her body wants something in it but the banana is rotten meat and rotten meat is just a stinking pile of shit to pile more shit onto the blob of shit that has enveloped her, the one she can't escape

71

again. She pulls out a jar of buttons and unscrews the lid.

This is disgusting. You're disgusting. But they look like little candies, so shiny, so colorful, so bright. She reaches in and takes out a handful of the things. She examines them hesitantly. This isn't normal. This isn't natural. It's disgusting. You are disgusting. Can't you just keep your fat, whorish mouth shut? Show some fucking self control. She's tearing up.

"I'm all fucked up. I'm fat and weird and I'm never going to be a doctor."

She takes a single delicate plastic pastiline and puts it into her mouth. It doesn't taste like candy. It tastes like plastic. It tastes like not food at all and that is what's appealing about it. She crunches down it hard and then again, until it shatters into several jagged pieces, which she gleefully gulps down. So seldom does she gleefully gulp anything down. She puts the jar away. She looks away from the mirror. She puts her shirt back on and opens up her book and goes back to studying.

The words turn into ants and crawl about. She blinks, looks down again. The words have turned to ants and crawl about. She closes the book. She closes her eyes and counts to 100 again as she tried to do with Julie. But Julie was there and the ants are there. She puts the book down. And once again she stares intently at the drawer. There's a jar in there of plastic pastilines and she is hungry.

# THE RAKE'S PROGRESS

It has been far too long. I cannot remember the name that was the name I had when I was a man. It was long ago, across the ocean in England. I was the man that I was. I was young and I was wealthy, I was spoiled and I was happy. I was happy enough but I was never what you would call "satisfied." Satisfaction is a thing hard won for any man be he rich or be he poor, weak or strong, I was rich and though I had riches, fine clothes and servants, rich foods and comfort, I had hungers like all men. They are nothing compared to the hungers I have now, but perhaps these were the hungers in their infancy.

Her name was Lisette. There was a her of course. A servant girl. Her hair was dark like Leah's, dark as Leah's. She was virtuous and kind and she adored me from afar, for I was finely dressed and healthy, my eyes were blue and clear and my hair was like spun gold. I looked perhaps like Micah's people once looked though without the peasant stock that chiseled some of the refinement from his face. She tried not to look at me. I know she tried not to look at me and I know that she failed. I in turn could not stop looking at her. That black in her hair was the black of the empty that I could never fill. She teased me with opacity. She made me think I could point out the spots where there was nothing but need and boredom. Two hundred fifty years and I still don't see them. I fill them best I can but I know nothing at all of their architecture.

At least I thought she had it in her to fill those parts. There is for every lack, every absence and every want, a soul to fill it. If there were not, then how could anyone call life fair? If the void cannot be filled and we are doomed to lack and absence, then the game is finished before it starts and there can be no reason for us to be born at all.

So one day I decided that I would speak my heart to her. As she sat by the river doing the wash, I joined her. I humbled myself to touch the garments of my family and the servants alike. And as I humbled my hands, I humbled my heart as well and told of her beauty and my want for her and even more my need and humbler still than that my desperation. I proclaimed my love with the skills I honed as a gentleman of letters and a poet. I was gifted with my words and brought tears to her eyes. And so we kissed. We embraced. And so I experienced the pleasures of the flesh and knew bliss. I could think of nothing so blissful as to be wed to my lovely Lisette. So I promised her we'd be wed.

We trysted often in my bed, in the woods, in the stables, anywhere we could get the privacy to explore our desires. It was all I needed. Until the day came as it always does when it no longer was. Her small flat bosoms felt inadequate in my hands. Her lips were no longer the softest and sweetest things I'd tasted. My love for Lisette was gone but my desire to better experience the deeper pleasures of the flesh was aflame. I went into town and I tried my luck and my poetry with other women. I began to ignore Lisette in favor of goldenhaired and redhaired women, women with great heaping tits and willing dripping innards.

Lisette became despondent and angry. She begged me to marry her as I had promised. She pleaded for me to love her again. When asked why she felt it was so urgent that I give my life to her again, she replied that she was pregnant with my child. Panic and disgust overcame me. The thought of caring and raising the weak and pasty whelp of some servant bitch that I no longer cared for drove me into a fit of rage. I slapped her in the face, I undressed her and not from love or lust but rage and hatred, I fucked her. I fucked her savagely, slapping her, biting her throat as hard as I could until I drew blood. I grew harder and hungrier for flesh than I ever had been and her cunt was sopping wet even as she begged for me to stop for the sake of my child.

I chomped down on her throat hard as I could but I didn't stop there, I turned her around and raped her purpled ass. Blood in my mouth, blood on my cock, a servant I'd claimed to love with my child inside her begging and struggling for her life, I had never experienced such ecstasies and felt as if I could not have truly lived before having had this. By the end of my work, the bitch of course was dead.

If she hadn't been dead when I ripped at her neck with my teeth, drawing my rapier and shoving it into her cunt would have done it. Rape and blood on my hands, the power to take a life, I felt for the first time ever what a splendid thing it was to be a man and to be the lord of one's domain. And I could not get enough of this now. My wealth and my cunning covered up the deaths of servants and whores, bodies used to death and then taken by me even after death had wrenched their souls from them. I used them until they began to rot and reek.

I had license to do as I pleased and I certainly did so, yet once again, I found myself lacking contentment. This is when I started to seek out books of occult import, books on alchemy, magic, conjurations, transmutations of elements and communing with the dead, the works of Dee and Paracelsus and Cyprian and Alhazred and their ilk. With the aid of these books, the barriers that still stood between me and ultimate potential were becoming only illusions.

I read voraciously, performed magical experiments but I found my results quite unsatisfactory. So, I had to seek out tutelage. So, I journeyed to Spain, the occult capital of Europe at the time. I followed rumors and bribes and dead men, I came upon The Black Academy at Salamanca, the secret school of dark magic that gave rise to Europe's foulest necromancers. I was a more than apt pupil at this place and had no trouble learning from them to commune with the dead, to influence men's hearts and call forth and hold court with the hosts of Hell itself.

I returned to my ancestral home a formidable sorcerer. I used my magic and my influence alike to enforce my will upon the townsfolk. With my will and my magic and my cock and my knife and my money and my servants and my infernal thirst, I was as unjust and wicked a lord as ever lived. What I do now for the poor souls inside my walls is a tender mercy in comparison.

But the day came, as it often does for witches, that pious men gathered and beat down my door, knocked me out, manacled me and put me before a judge and sentenced me to burn. I did nothing to deny their accusations, as I took much pride in them and felt certain that my arcane benefactors would aid me in my last moments, swooping down and freeing me on demon wings and bearing me elsewhere. Of course, I had no reason to trust in demons as nobody should. My last sensations were nothing but agony. In spite of all I'd done, all I have done, you must pity wretched me.

The very flesh was melted from my bones, then the bones themselves were charred until they crumbled to dust. The demons did nothing for me but to let me feel and bear witness to this until at last I was done with being. With all the horrors and dark experiments I had witnessed at The Black Academy, still nothing compared to that feeling of my body and all I was melting away as gathered apostates laughed and jeered at the last moments of the witch that had plagued them. The last words I uttered, screamed as my very mouth faded from existence were a curse on the judge who had done this to me. The judge's family fled to America and built this house, a house where I held dominion in the walls.

Of course, that story is a lie. I am not so transparent or giving with my mysteries. This is the dream and the hunch I send Brian. In his heart, he knows me as this warlock, though he has not put it together.

Though one part of the story is certainly true: when I am bored, I do terrible things.

# TOGETHER

"I'm afraid," says Micah, staring up at the ceiling. "I feel different sometimes lately. Like I'm not myself."

Cytherea clasps his hand.

"Like you're somebody else?"

Of course, that's what he means you fucking cunty cow. Of course that's what he fucking means. If he isn't him, he's clearly someone else. She is concerned though. She is actually concerned, for some reason she's concerned about him. She has felt the violence, she has felt the thing thrashing, she has felt the worst in her come climbing up as well, she has felt it. But of course it means he feels like someone else. He will be nobody. He will be mine. He is mine. He will be mine. I look in him and wonder what I value and I honestly can't find it but the fact is that it doesn't matter what. The Closetsong is out there and it wants to make me quiet.

"I keep having dreams," he says, "and I never feel in control when I have these dreams. I'm someplace dark. I'm in the woods."

"You're someplace dark," she says, making circles on his chest, "you're in the woods."

"Deeper. Darker. Not like in the literal woods. Like in some kind of you know, like astral woods. Like a Happy Hunting Ground or something. Like there's one woods where everyone gets lost and I've stumbled away from civilization and I'm lost in those woods. Like Hansel and Gretel or Little Red Ridinghood. There are old faerie things in there. Maybe I've been whisked off to faerie. It could be. Maybe I've gotten too connected to this place, to the Earth."

She kisses him, trying to suck the grief through his

mouth, watching his eyes flutter. I can see it work. I want to burn the Earth just to snuff out the secrets of why. I will suck everything there is into my walls until I can tear it apart and see. What's joy is not joy. What's hope is not hope. Why must I walk in circles when I've eternity to roam? Does the Closetsong know? Can I suck it from the marrow in its spirit?

"You are powerful," she says, "you are attuned. And you are beautiful."

She kisses his chest, draws his nipples into her mouth, toying with them in her teeth, hardening them as he so often draws hers out. Maddy wants her to bite down, shred them, spurt out blood. I agree with Maddy. It seems like a good idea. But I can't. Maybe I just won't. What is being done to me? What is being done to this space? Shall I open my toybox and yank off limbs until someone knows the answer? Someone knows? Doctorpuppet must be plotting. Maddy and I are getting along. Antonia seems so innocent. It could be Antonia. She has some power over me, over them. Ungrateful little cunt—it must be her. I want to rip it open and see what makes me treasure it. I would mock them for their dull quaint notions of value.

He is moaning. He is happy. He is frightened. He is wise to be afraid. He is stirring. I am stirring. I am stirring in him. He wants her to stop. I don't. He wants her to keep going. I do too. Should not stop.

"There's something in those woods. Whether it's out there or it's in me, I don't know."

"You're strong. You're beautiful and attuned. You don't need to be scared, Micah. You can trust it. I trust you and I love you, Micah. It's something wonderful in you and it's growing. You need to trust the forest. And your instincts. Always trust your instincts."

She keeps trailing down his belly. There is something distant and different in her voice. Something big, distant and wise. Or very very foolish. She's not on drugs. She's not

alone. The me in her and the Maddy in her are not alone.
I do not care whose interests you'd maintain, they are not
mine since it is not me engaging them. I do not care whose
interests you maintain, you'll be gone from here. I do not care
what you make of this house and what it could be. I do not
care what you make of this house and what you can do for it.
The Closetsong is speaking through her. I consider moving
straight away. It would expect that. I hear you hearing me
you rotten shit I hear you hearing me!

I am louder than Closetsong. I am a tune behind tunes
and it must not forget.

Cytherea keeps kissing down, pulls down his shorts and
pulls him out, gives it a feathery touch with her lips to call
it out of hiding. To coax me out of hiding just as likely. I
hear you hearing me I can predict this outmaneuver you and
triumph. I only triumph. Hollow. Hollow victories. More
hollow things. I could drop a pin in the things I've won and
it would sound like thunder.

What is this doubt, this misstep? I had to have been here
before. I am timeless. I flutter into him as she starts to kiss
and suck, tender and enthusiastic in her hunger. I feel him
feeling nothing but her mouth and fill his nostrils with the
musk of Pan. The musk of Pan pervading, he tries to make
me go. He dares to try and make me go. I have gotten lax. No
more. No more distraction. What if there is no Closetsong?
What if doubt is a force that emerges when you near perfect?
I have dismantled hearts with doubt. Perhaps I've collected
too much.

He throws her down, her reaches to the floor and in one
swift, talented motion, he pulls the belt from his pants, he
wraps it around her throat. She complies and smiles.

"Yes, it's something beautiful. You need to learn to trust
the woods."

And he does. He trusts the musk and the woods and
trusts me and not the smarmy shit who thinks he can take

them away or else take them better. These walls belong to me. Her cunt belongs to me. He proves it with all his might as he thrusts in and pulls the belt. Thrust yank thrust yank thrust yank thrust yank. She is starting to slip, she is starting to move toward me. Is it too soon? I cannot quite feel if I care. He pounds her fierce and brutal. He writes "MINE" in her womb. And she is but me means me. The only me is me. When will they see?

She gets glassy and gasps, she gets terribly faint, a wheeze, a whisper, a loss. I can feel her etheric hand pull toward me then away. I overestimate what's mine and how complete. She's pulling away and into life. She pushes him off, a wild werewolf smile on her face and with all her might, she frees herself from the belt and makes it hers. And around his throat it goes and she pulls and it feels good. They play this game. She takes his cock and pumps and pumps and pumps, exploding gouts of cum. It begins to fold up and go but her mouth won't let this happen. She sucks it big again. She sucks it triumphant and sits on it and bounces and she squeezes his throat with the belt. The squeezes are short and rhythmic, the breath played like a piano. She only wants certain sounds. She wants to play along with the Closetsong and it sounds so sweet it hurts me.

I haven't a throat for teeth but I feel its teeth on my throat and it hasn't a throat for teeth and I haven't teeth but it, it still feels mine. The whatever we are pushes against each other, united in violence like the lovers we puppeteer. Has it come here to love me? Does it bring an understanding of love? Is it the notion that I could love myself? What are you? I know you taste like a taste and that taste is something good. You infringe on me corrupt my walls, sing inside my closets, violator! I want you to stop right now. Then I want you to start again and I want you to corrupt my walls as he is corrupting hers. This is the hardest I've been pushed against, the biggest prerogative I know. It sprays something unknowable in my throat. I cannot explain metaphysics. Not my role. Not me.

They still choke and fuck without us. There are reassuring strokes from her hand on his cheek. And I am pushing up against it, it makes itself known. It will be well. Why can't you trust me? Don't you know it will be well?

"Don't listen!" Maddy shrieks, "you're stronger than this. Do you need someone to love you? I can love you! See the glass I grind inside me? I can love you. But you can't let this make you weak."

I feel weary. I feel deceived. I feel the teeth of whatever it is on whatever in me is like my throat. I feel the intruder in my walls. Though it woos me by seeing my bidding done, I know intrusion when I smell it and I cannot welcome it as Cytherea welcomes Micah into hers, bouncing rhythmic, reassuring, choking slowly, leaning in to kiss in and steal more breath, careful to spare her rhythm so he doesn't breathe too heavy. I wish he'd breathe too heavy though it's not yet time. I always want to say I know what's mine.

I withdraw slightly from the consciousnesses at hand, reward Maddy for her intervention with a journey back to some of her most exquisite moments torturing Antonia. She is squatting above the girl, taking a great long shit on the porcelain face beneath her as Doctorpuppet sits on a chair and smiles, masturbating furious and hard. Antonia is trying to object but stops herself. She knows that worse is ahead if she does, not realizing that death would be better even though death won't be better not when my arms are open to all of this, open to owning the things that pass the threshold. The stench of rotten meats and cheeses long gone almost drown the girl. But she opens her mouth and swallows, tastes damnation again, trying not to choke like Leah with her fat.

For Maddy this is paradise. Maddy has been good to me this time, the kind of good, the rare, nigh nonexistent kind of good that resides in a rare putrid heart like Maddy's. I

81

sit and watch with Maddy, trying to experience the thing that feels like pleasure to me through the suffering of Antonia who is mine. I cannot find the fervor in Clarence. I am calling Doctorpuppet Clarence. I look around in the past, the chamber set aside and in this place, I can't hear the Closetsong.

I drag Maddy back to champagnecunt, to Antonia's triumph and feel the thing like pleasure. I feel a great deal of the thing like pleasure. Maddy feels betrayed. Maddy feels betrayed because I might have been.

"You stay here," I hiss through all that makes her up, "you stay here until you tell me. You tell me what it is. Tell me about the sounds from the closets."

"I hear it but I don't know what it is or what you mean. What do you mean?" her voice is faint. She is not at all like Maddy. She is tiny. She is a child over her father's knee again. She is begging. Antonia is sliding the bottle in and out. Maddy is bleeding and I'm making it real real slow. Champagnecunt at half speed. Begging and screaming and triumph lasting all the longer. I search her and I wonder if the Closetsong can hide things inside of people like it hides inside the walls to do inscrutable things, things that deceive and hurt me. I will not be fooled. I am far too old and powerful and smart for that.

"I don't believe you," I say, pulling back Antonia's arm and slowing it to a speed that can only be called glacial. The strike ferments for centuries before it is executed, slowly, mightily and cruelly so. She screams for an eternity but none of these screams are my answer. I leave her there to stew and maybe she will be more cooperative. Or else she won't. I don't care.

I return to the room and Micah's legs are in the air. Cytherea, smile upon her face, is easing a finger into the ass I claimed as Pan. I have seen them do this. I have seen this blissful grin. Their bliss is of no consequence to me.

I could abandon the scene but it has been here. Leah is weeping through the night. There is nothing to do with Leah. She is mine. Kaz and Brian might go into that room and Leah will do them no harm and that's all well and good. The harm is coming and it will make them mine. But this, this is something to sit and watch. Am I like Clarence on his little chair as his wife squats on precious Antonia?

Micah moans, eyes locked in those of his lover, eyes drowning in those of his lover. Their closeness is not always apparent but right now it is clear as clear can be. There is no more denying what they are or fighting against it right now. So, I leave them be. I whisper that I am in the room but do no more to color or shape their intimacies. They barely hear me and they barely care. She fingerfucks him with the utmost care, acknowledging what he is to her each movement. I witness so many intimacies and I want to get it. I get it, I have so many hearts and essences to make inquiries in. Have they come up short?

He moves into her, trusting someone who so often he thinks betrays him, who so often does betray him, who keeps so many secrets in uglies all over her. He moves into her and accepts her completely as she accepted him completely, as the mine accepts me completely. Doctorpuppet knocks, Clarence and asks if he can sit beside me and watch. Is he seeing me unravel. He is seeing me unravel. Can't be trusted. Never could. That's how he's mine. I could deny him but I keep him close and he watches with me, breathing heavy into the room. Micah turns his head thinking he's heard something then withdraws from the thought and back into the touch of his lover.

She gingerly slides in a second finger, challenging the architecture of prostate. Wriggling round, she animates him more, increases the volume of his moans. Micah's head shakes whipping his long blonde hair back and forth. Don't stop don't stop don't stop don't stop his manhood is hard implacable a peak at a peak. Why am I so interested in this? The workings of these bedrooms? What should anyone care about the workings of these bedrooms? They argue for it. His spasms of joy explain it again. So often they explain it and so often I return to watch this. The prettiest and ugliest of their behaviors. A dot of "yes" congeals upon the tip.

The third finger does not go in so easy. The third one is rapid and intense. She has pulled out the two and added the third abruptly. What is this? This seems like something I'd tell her to do or like something something like me would tell me to do. There is only one thing like me and that is me or there are two things like me and that is it. I like this, what she is doing, I like this, it's right but I have to stop her, I rush toward her, I rush into her and call out for the intruder but the intruder can't be found but she is still going, smile big, she is laughing and he is saying stop and trying to wriggle away like she had been but he cannot wriggle away, he has gotten weak and sleepy and she is strong she is suddenly so strong all things rerouted all blood recirculated into this invasive act. He is in pleasure, he is agony. He knows what this is like. This is justice. There should be no justice in fucking. It should be inherently fair, I have watched it so much, it should be inherently fair. This isn't fair. Out out stop! Out out stop!

A fourth. He is crying out. He is screaming. Brian and Kaz should be able to hear but they know not to intervene when there are screams from this room. There are so often screams from this room that it is known as a place where screaming happens. This is a place where screaming happens. They are a place where screaming happens. He is a place where screaming happens and he wants her out. She is smiling she is giggling she is not listening she is elsewhere even as I look around inside her and try to find the song.

"Let her go! I scream at it! You'll ruin this!"

It does not let her go. It does not listen. It slides her hand inside him and makes a fist and he is wide and he is suffering and he is cumming and he wants for her to stop and he screams for her to stop and he tries to find the word help but someone has stolen it from him. I cannot give it back. I am not in control. I am not in control here. Of me of them I am not in control here and I cannot let this be. You let him go. You let him go. You let her go. My pleas are inconsequential as their had been to me.

"What is this?" I ask.

It looks at me through Cytherea's eyes and Cytherea's grin and it speaks, the first words I've heard from it.

"You think you know of houses, you know nothing of houses. You only know of this house. There are so very many houses, wallsgod. I am here to help you. Acknowledge my beauty and strength and I will help you."

"I won't!" I hiss through Micah's lips, asserting myself to slide him off of her and back on top of her. He takes the belt and shows her tits what's what. He takes his cock and shows her insides what's what, shoots her full of everything in his balls. It leaves and I leave and we leave them to wonder about the places where people scream.

# PLAYING DOCTOR

Leah has drawn the circles. She is nervous again, shirt off, looking at her work. She sighs.

"I don't know."

Julie puts a hand on Leah's shoulder.

"I think you look great just the way you are."

And Julie knows that's the worst she can say to her. She knows that Leah will think her feelings are being protected and if her feelings are being protected then what are they being protected from and why? Why are they being protected? If the way to her heart is open, then why is it vulnerable? There must be something she's being spared. There can be just one thing she's being spared. She's been taking poor care of her body. She's getting big. She has to be getting big. And these, they're so thick and lumpy and ugly. Everyone thinks she's lean and slick beneath the sweatshirts and sweaters.

"Can you hand me the scalpel?" says Leah.

"You know you don't have to do this."

But she does.

"I know. I don't like this. I want it to stop."

Julie says nothing. I can feel the anguish in her knowing that she must stay silent. I don't understand this. She'll get Leah back she can be with Leah everywhere if she just listens. Julie is sentimental, unlike me. I am never sentimental. I love nostalgia but I am never sentimental. She doesn't want for it to be like this. She wants to see Leah happy now and free. That'll never happen. She is so much mine already.

She hands Leah the scalpel. The ingrate pleads that this just isn't right and that I don't need this woman. If she's so irrelevant, then why then is she loved? I'm not deceived.

Julie can see that she must be good now so she hands Leah the scalpel. How much could Julie really have cared for her? Melodrama. Nothing but melodrama. As she hands over the weapon, it becomes clear where her loyalties lie. You were never loyal to anyone. You never loved her. You don't care for these people at all. You should be grateful I let you betray them. You never had the courage to do it yourself now did you?

Leah makes the first incision. Ribbons of red. A smile. A semicircle. She bites her tongue, swallows copper, swallows hurt. She grabs the flask. She grabs the pills. She knows she'll have to make the cut before they've done their business all the way. She swallows her scream. It will be worth it. What's important is that she's the best Leah she can be and the best Leah is unburdened by sacks of rancid gravy. Julie begs me to let her let her stop. I will not let her let stop. I have Julie and Julie has nothing to give me. She is fighting to say please stop this, she is fighting to say this is crazy. But she can't say this is crazy. It can't be.

She keeps cutting. Deeper, more thorough. Hurts so much it makes them quiet, stiff. It tells them they have nothing to look forward to. She doesn't really know anyone with much to look forward to, not in school, not in this house. The cuts should be clean but her heart, her movements and motives aren't, she goes too deep, a spray and then suddenly ragged tearing. She'll never be a doctor. Lets the feelings get in the way.

"Leah, please..." says Julie, though just ahead I am showing her the oven and showing her the moments when we were at play and reminding her whose she is. I could take her there but I actually don't want to because being here will be worse for her and being here will educate her and she needs to be educated.

But the cuts are made, the strands of flesh and muscle that keep the breast in place have been completely severed. With her ungloved hand, she grabs the lump of now incoherent skin, squeezes, squeezes tighter and she pulls. She tosses the skin unceremoniously to the ground. She never cared for it. It wasn't her. And behind the skin she finds the source of offense, adipose, detritus, bullshit. And she grabs onto a handful of tacky, amorphous yellow Leah, examining it almost in disbelief. Was this her? It wasn't. And if it was, it can't be anymore. It's alien, it's wrong and yet she takes in my whispers, listens to the ideas I present and knows what to do with the objectionable outsider ooze.

She shovels the little lump of tissue into her mouth, chews on it. She savors it. She almost contemplates what she's missing. She's thinking of food. Good. She can think of food again. Salt. Rust. Meat. Sugar. Salt. Rust. Meat. Sugar. She closes her eyes and imagines it isn't her. She chews, savors and tries to down the lump of fat. She feels relieved, ecstatic, almost. She opens her eyes and looks again at all the ooze and oil before her and there is only one thing she can do. She reaches down into the carved breast, taking another mound of bloody fat and putting it into her delicate mouth.

She takes another lump and chews on it. She hasn't quite swallowed the first one; her mouth's still full. She chokes and sobs ashamed that she can't resist this, ashamed of being in that cold, dark basement between exhale and choke, between the body she thinks she has and the one she does, between herself and the topheavy freakish thing that she's ashamed of are clearer then they've ever been.

"You can eat now, Leah," says Julie, feeling me feel around her soul and twist and stretch and rip at it and remind her I am there. Leah sobs and nods and shovels more into her mouth. She chokes some,. tears dripping down her face, inarticulate pain, moans stifled, questions. She is cutting again. Deep as before, now trembling, now hitting some of the wrong nerves, now pooling more blood, chewing, sobbing, cutting, bleeding, begging. The second breast is tossed again to the floor, again exposing blood and yellow rusty grime.

"How does it taste, Leah? How do you taste?"

On phantom strings I drag her to her friend, she tries to pull away but stops and thinks about how she's mine already and there's no resisting and there will be nothing but punishment for more time than she can imagine. She puts her hand over Leah's mouth and pushes, shoving the fat back down her throat. She tries to cough and choke and gasp and fails. Julie reaches behind the severed bosom and grabs a heaping handful. Leah, my Leah, lost Leah, sad Leah soon to be dead Leah does something that shocks even me.

She opens her mouth and lets her old friend feed her, lets the girl she loved feed her. She shoves the bloodied yellow rot into poor Leah's mouth, which she covers again, lets her chew and bleed and swallow and sob and cry. Leah is gasping, Leah is dizzy, Leah is bloodied, Leah is mine, Leah is panicking, Leah is peaceful, Leah is breathless, Leah is dead.

# HIDE AND SEEK

I do not understand what it's showing me. A boy of five. A boy I do not know. He is trembling in a closet, curled up in a nest of dress shirts, clutching them tight. His eyes are closed. He is mumbling what might be a prayer. Creeping up behind him is a man in a charcoal grey suit that is practically forged of creases. His face is dusty dead caved in by time, eyes gone, there are only grubs and flies behind them. All that there is of skin clings tight as virgins and nothing at all about it looks like skin. He stands behind the boy just breathing and even though his eyes are closed the child knows what is that stands behind him.

A clump of maggots from behind the empty eyes falls down to the child's shoulder. The little white dashes and tildes crawl from the child's shoulder up his neck. The man in charcoal grey whispers to the boy, speaking through the squirming things.

"If you start to scream, you stay in here forever."

The boy reaches out for the door, the door that has become a wall.

"I wasn't the one," man in charcoal grey, "I didn't lock you in here, so you can't get out. You'll see sunlight says the when it's time."

Behind him there are sounds. High pitched howls like those of monkeys. Augmented bark of distant dog. Slow motion laughter, humorless wintery. A choir of baritone voices. Empty empty gone no no no empty empty gone no no no...

There is poetry in all of this. Never seen the workings of children. Fragile and trusting. But if you lock grown men in closets, they would scream and try to beat down the door This child holds his tongue and prays for sunlight, prays for out. Though this world is only scream and dark and rot, the boy stands firm. The maggot crawls up his face, to the edge of his ear and whispers right into the drum speaking into it, breathing out digested reek from the man in charcoal grey.

"There will be ways to forget this," says the charcoal grey corpse through the maggot, "and one day, you can make it so you won't have to sit in dark and wait for sunlight. Look back to this and the way out opens up. The world is full of bottles, scalpels, pills."

But then, as the closet door opens into a day twenty five years gone, the light that he has begged for brings me clarity. I see now the face of the foe and closets and cadavers are the least of it.

# HOMONCULUS

Kaz is feeling fuzzy and strange. She is forgetting a great deal. She is in bed and alone and confused. Something is happening to her, an enigma wide as the stars. Something is happening and she doesn't know where it came from.

"Come back," says Kaz, not knowing to whom she's speaking. The words are alien but the only right ones in the situation.

"Come back here, you bastard!"

She is the size of the Earth and the sky, if she yawned and stretched she would occupy all of time. And she can feel it. She is not expanding. The flesh she had is stretched out and there will only be so much of it but she feels as if she will only find out about it when she runs out. She doesn't know who she's calling out to or what he has done to her but she would kill whoever it was. I offer some reassurance. I feel tender toward her. The Closetsong is polluting me. It's poisonous like that. I will cease to be me if I cannot be rid of it. I offer some reassurance. She looks up into the face of the roommate she had shunned so often. Leah places a hand on her forehead, strokes her hair.

"Don't worry," she says with a smile, "we're here."

"We?" says Kaz, quivering from the thing swimming inside her and pushing against her stomach to make its way out and the pain of it punching her in the womb simply because it can. It pushes on her simply because it can.

And there is Julie. The girl who went has suddenly come back. Strawberry blonde glimmer, yellow sundress, mary janes and delight. Everybody had loved Julie a little bit. Lucky Kaz, here was Julie again, reaching out and squeezing her hand. There is no reason for her to be here but there is no reason for her to be gone so Kaz is filled with joy at her two dead midwives.

"Thank you for coming," says Kaz, "I've missed you."

"I wouldn't miss it for the world," says Julie, "congratulations. Who's the lucky guy?"

Kaz lets out a piercing shriek. The statement is perhaps accurate. She doesn't know who it is, what it is. There are no words. It pounds against her as she screams. It is screaming too. It is screaming "why?," it is screaming "help me" and "out," most of all, it is screaming "out." Soon. Julie puts her hand on the bump, massages it as it moves. Antonia appears in the corner of the room, gold and beatific. She smiles as Julie has smiled. Kaz has seen this girl and has not seen her. She brings her comfort though and joy delight, like Julie, delight. It almost quiets the pain. Almost.

"It's coming soon," says Julie.

"Are you doing okay?" asks Leah, "Let me know if you need anything. I'm going to be a doctor someday."

A tear appears on Leah's cheek.

"It will be so nice. With an office with my name over the door. Mom and dad will be so proud. You don't need to worry, Kaz, I can help you."

"Something's wrong, Leah," Kaz mumbles, "something's not right here."

"All expectant mothers think that. Don't you worry, I'm going to be a doctor."

"Leah, you're not a doctor. And something's wrong with you..."

There are two great big red circles pooling up on Leah's sweatshirt, dripping out the chest. Leah does not acknowledge them at all, nor does anyone else in the room. Something is terribly wrong. Her body begins to twitch and expand. She feels herself being stretched into a great tundra of flesh. She feels she must be the bigger than the room and the house even. The room elongates from study to a hallway, time and space stretching out as Kaz's body does. Leah and Julie have hold of her legs and they are pulling them, with a strength that just doesn't seem right for their size. Nothing about this is right.

Doctorpuppet appears beside her. He is ruffling her hair as Leah and Julie extend her legs far beyond their capabilities, long, skinny, feeling almost infinite. She is feeling almost infinite and this thing is shaking inside her and Doctorpuppet is ruffling her hair.

"Shh, shh, it's okay. Don't worry. I've got something to tell you, Kaz…"

Kaz lets out a scream loud enough for an entire species wiped from the Earth by tides or comets or volcanic ash. Kaz lets out a scream that should explode her lungs, destroy her ribs from impact and send bony shrapnel all the way down this corridor that the study is becoming for no good reason, or at least in Kaz's mind for no good reason. Doctorpuppet waits until the shrieking stops.

"Kaz, I've betrayed you. I'm not a very good doctor."

"I am!" says Leah gleefully, stretching Kaz out as far as she has needed to be stretched at last. A bunch like the martialed meals of her entire life trying to make their way out, squirming out towards her towards her towards her…

Kaz realizes and shrieks. She knows at last. She sees the face of the father and the culprit. Knows the thing the Closetsong wanted her to get rid of, feels the prophetic thunders of its coming out her body, a body that surely cannot stand this, a body that must have been stretched and used and abused to its very limits that must surely be spent forever. She stops shrieking when she thinks this might be the end. The hand of Doctorpuppet on her forehead does no good.

Maddy appearing and screaming out epiphets like "Whore!" and "Jezebel!" and monsters makes the thing inside her only squirm worse and make its journey hard as it can make it. Her womb comes tunneled through, her sex expands like her legs, widens out, a great red, pink funnel. She feels something round and her beating against her entrance.

"You look so beautiful," says Leah, "fat and gross for certain. All fat. But there's something about you now, you know, a glow. Do you feel the glow? Do you feel all warm inside? I never got to be a mother."

Leah begins to sob, so loud, so hard, so out of control she starts to sound less like a person and more like an animal in pain.

"I never got to be a mother but at least I get to be a doctor. It's not fair though. I should have had everything. They told me I could have it all and I worked so hard!"

"Whore! Jezebel!" shouts Maddy, "You fat, disgusting monster!"

"So fat," hisses Leah, "so disgusting. Such a fucking whore!"

"Stop it!" shouts Doctorpuppet, "she doesn't need this right now, you selfish cunts."

"SEL-FISH CUNT!" screams Maddy.

"I'm being torn up," says Kaz, "I'm going to die now."

Leah gives Kaz the finger.

"Fuck you! Fuck your drama! You're always like this!"

Leah's mood swings back as she looks between Kaz's vastly expanded legs. There is something red and spherical emerging. Leah and Julie approach, suddenly a spring in their steps. Kaz shrieks and shrieks and shrieks. The two girls grab hold of the sides of the great emerging ball that rips Kaz more.

"I'm sorry, Kaz, I'm such a bad doctor," says Doctorpuppet, "this is my fault. I shouldn't have done that."

"Whore!"

The two pull on the corners of the great red ball, expanding

95

the red, pink shining hole that Kaz had used so badly for so long and revealing the nature of the object. It is a head, the head of the thing that squirmed and hated and writhed in her. It is hard to tell that it is at first because the thing lacks eyes and where its nose should be is just a skull like indentation. The head is red and slick with blood and amniotic fluids. Its mouth already toothy only opens halfway, half sealed shut by a glob of flesh. It is bigger than a grown man's head. The infant coming out of her is far far larger than her and bigger than any grown man she has ever seen.

Julie and Leah pull on its broad but slumped down shoulders. It has no neck. It is hard to tell how it could swallow anything. Its arms are long and spindly, ending in hands that have not fingers but five scalpels, long gangly, apelike arms ending in fatal blades. She shrieks and shrieks some more as she sees the thing emerge, emaciated, sunken chest next, then sloping pelvis.

Between its legs is a member larger than any she has ever seen, clearly over a foot long and at the end of it not the head she's used to. At the end of that long, ropy shaft is a round, cherubic face, the face of a sleeping infant. It sleeps between the gangly subhuman legs of the mutation, legs like a kangaroo. Leah and Julie do not lie it down anywhere, choosing instead to prop it up.

It stumbles like a foal on those legs, with the slopes and lopsides of its malformed body. But it stands successfully. Kaz sees the thing doesn't take long to successfully render itself upright. At her feet is a great puddle of blood and placenta and things she did not even know could have been in her. She has been rendered vast and forced to exalt and suffer in her vastness.

"Kill it!" the ripped up, giant Kaz screams to her roommate and her former roommate, both dead, "You can't let that thing live."

"You say that now," says Doctorpuppet, "and it's only

natural. Mothers always feel this way about their children. It's always stressful to experience separation from one's infant. You need to look at the big picture."

"Kill it! It's a monster! It's killed me!"

"Glowing. That's it. You're glowing."

"I'm going to die," she mumbles.

All are startled, living and dead when the head at the end of the infant's member opens its mouth.

"Mother, you need not panic. You have sought unconditional love your whole life and have been met with only treason and abuse. That shall be no more. I will love you, mother, I will fight for you."

She stands up, suddenly finding her body knitting itself together again. She approaches her child, hugs him, then kisses the face on the lips.

# MARIONETTE

"I don't want to do this," she says, sitting on a stool in the basement facing the wall. Antonia is being uncooperative, so I have brought her someplace bad. History's the scourge, these moments the lash. When I say that I am god within these walls, it is because no gods could touch them save for me. I have scraped those papery hearts for signs of some communion with something old and big and gentle and sensible and in them I have found only imagined footsteps down the hallway and a choir of silences where there really should be voices. And in these walls, in the cold impenetrable timetomb, the voice, the one voice is me. There are worse places I can take her and she knows it. So she'll comply. When you cross this threshold, there is nobody else to talk to.

"I can't do this," she says to the wall, "it's not right."

Her objections are strong, as they should be. I treasure her for a reason. I am not sentimental but I am very sentimental toward Antonia. It must be done. She is the one that he will let in. He hasn't seen her yet, I do not think. But he felt her basement, he feels her down there and he is reaching, always reaching for her hand, even though he knows nothing of her hand or the woman that it belongs to. There is something there he wants to feel again. I smell that need. I will be generous, compliant. I am a just loving god though I might not seem like a just and loving god. I won't be judged. Gods won't be judged.

"You've been good to me," she says to the eternal corner, "you saved me from them. You were kind and in your way, you were loving. I want to do right by you and I wish that I was what you want me to be."

The Closetsong is getting to me. The Closetsong has reached

me. I want to tell her she's perfect. Why should I tell her she's perfect? She's mine, she's part of me. I do not need to tell her that she's perfect. I do not need to tell that she pleases me. She displeases me. This displeases me. I need them and I need to have them. They have crossed my threshold, they are rightful mine. She is rightful mine and my things can't be insubordinate. I cannot let this be. I want to tell her she's perfect. It could hurt her to tell her she's perfect and I can't hurt her but I can only hurt her.

"I want you to know that I appreciate all of this and I know you're doing what you think is right. I don't know what you are and I don't know if you know but I know you have to do this," she says to the eternal corner even as she starts to sob. I seldom stopped to object to tears before but I object to tears.

I wish to lift her from the eternal corner, pull arms from the ether and wrap them around her. The Closetsong makes me think like this. Makes me stop and feel. It is native to another place and so it makes me look outside me and what is outside me but the insides of those inside me? I want to console her but I cannot because I need those who crossed the threshold. But it's alright because when I have them it will leave me be. What can it do then but leave me be? I am thinking in circles. I must stay sharp. I must let her cry.

"But they hurt me," she says, "they hurt me so bad. And how do I know these others won't? You're God maybe. You know what's best. I'll help you. I'm sorry. I love you and I want to help you."

This is so. This is right. This is the thing I treasure. This is the finest of them.

I waft her in, a thing of essence, perfume. I waft her through the air in his room. She is on the wind now, riding into his nose as he sleeps, into his brain, flickering into dream. He can feel her hurt, what was done. He knows she was done wrong, even though he knows not what she is. He knows her as a scent in a field in a dream. He knows her as roses and meat and hot and joyous. If he were awake, he would know she was what he felt in the basement. So I shake him awake.

His eyes and his nose and his thumping heart open. He breathes deep and wants to cry. This thing was not, this thing like him, this thing he likes, it just wasn't. But I pull away the veil between "there" and "gone" and when it's pulled away there shimmers into sight dear dirty blonde Antonia. Antonia is wearing nothing as she did when she served other masters. Her high, conical breasts, her clean shaved sex, her leanness, the inward curve of her hip, her permissive smile are all there to know and absorb. The there is incontrovertible.

"I've felt you before," he says, "I didn't think you were there."

"I've been there," she says, "I watch you. I like you. I watched you with her. I wasn't jealous."

"What's your name?" he asks.

"Antonia. You're Brian?"

He nods. She gets up on her knees and advances up his body, standing above him like he's something she has vanquished. Not yet but she is on the way. The slave is so proud, strong and confident right now. This being who has been literally shat on quite often is completely in control.

"Would you like to kiss me, Brian?"

"I don't know you."

"You didn't answer my question."

"Yes," he says breathlessly, "yes, I want to kiss you."

She kisses him. She delicately grazes his thigh with her leg and these things are enough to make him hard for her straight away. The dead girl makes his body surge with life. She uses the gift of shape and solid, the gift of skinagain well. There are reasons I treasure her so. He will grow to treasure her too. She pulls away from the kiss, brushes a second time against his lips but does not complete the kiss.

"Do you like it when I kiss you?"

She learned this under the lash and in the corner. The taste of Maddy's shit clumping in the back of her throat taught her all there is to know about delicacy, subtlety and tact. And she says it through this almost-a-kiss. His body is shaking, shocked. It cannot help but tell that something is as wrong with this as it is so very right. But does he like it when she kisses him? The right and wrong are very insubstantial in this matter.

"Yes," he says. It was almost "of course" because the wispy nymph is clearly an of course. He grabs her entire buttocks, honed by thrusting and starving, in a palm and a half. He's bold. She puts the lips that shockwaved through him on his throat. She sucks the flesh so slightly it's almost just a breath in but if she held her breath, if she gave her all, she could drink it like an ocean, making suck up the whole of him. A sucking, a half inhale, a graze of teeth. Withdraw, then travel down, withdraw then taste a moment. Withdraw and make him want much more. She tickles his chest with a strand of her dirty blonde hair that swings over him like a silent windchime.

Then she leans in, tasting his earlobe ever so slightly.

"They beat me. They pissed on me and shat in my mouth. They choked me with belts. Whipped me. Fucked me in the ass 'til I bled. Used the blood for lube. Do you want to hit me? Wanna choke me? Fuck me in the ass I bleed? Do you want that?"

"No." Part of him is lying. It is in the nature of these creatures to lie. He hasn't done these things but he would really like to know.

She kisses his chest, biting his nipple, reaches down into his boxers and begins to toy with his balls.

"I like you, Brian. You deserve to have what you want."

He knows full well he's not perfect but he feels right now like he might be.

"Get on top."

"If that's what you want," she says, deftly yanking off his underwear. She lowers herself onto him slowly, letting each inch of him, each angle know how it feels to be in her. He fits into her like a glove and she squeezes him so tight and tender

101

as he does. She sits still, doesn't start moving, lets him just see what it feels like to be in her and know her. She bounces just once. Then again. She brushes her hand against his cheek.

"Is this what you want?" she asks, "I like you."

He can only nod. I feel him opening to me a little, vulnerable, his mind knowing that he had been presented a gift by someone powerful and glorious and infinitely larger than him. He has had girls before but not like this. He was popular a bit for his guitar and for his hair and his sort of good looks. He was popular for his dark clothes and his time spent in quiet corners. But he has not had this. He has not seen anything this compliant or loving. The Closetsong is opening him some as if it wishes to be sporting, as if it thinks it's helping. And then of course all I can get is how wonderful she feels, how good she smells how real she is, how silly his denials. She is picking up her pace, she is swirling her hips and he is controlling her with his hands.

"I like you," he sighs.

"I like you too. Be calm. Enjoy this."

If there were questions, they've disappeared inside her with his cock.

"You're so beautiful, Antonia."

She feels a jolt of me in her, a jolt of shock. She knows what comes next. She knows what I brought her for. She knows what she objected to that led her to facing a corner for an eternity. She doesn't want to say it but she loves me for what I've given her, this power and eternal life, this glory and beauty and a chance to be bigger than people. She doesn't want to say it but she knows the consequences and she knows what happens when she doesn't eat the words that I have fed her. Even if she had loved this man more deeply than life itself, she would have a hard time resisting.

"You like me?"

"Yes."

"You like this?" She tenses her body, she pushes down

on him hard, works him fiercely.

"Yes."

"What if I was never here?" she asks, hips pounding like a hammer.

"I don't..." there is fear in his eyes though the rest of his body's delighted.

"What if I was dead? What if I was a murderer? A dead girl who killed a woman then was killed by her lover, or a man who thought he was her lover but was just her captor?"

"Why are you asking this?"

Suddenly laughter, laughter that shakes the world beyond their fucking. Laughter that can capsize him, drown him.

"I was never here," she says, letting her face rot away and drip onto his sheets, letting her face become like the face of the First Girl.

"You're crazy. Nothing happened, I was never here."

He tries to wiggle away from her but there is no escape. Her muscles are strong. They are my muscles and in these walls, I am god. To wiggle out the cunt of god cannot be done. He is exploding into her as her rotted face looks down on him in judgment, asserting absence and whispering gone gone gone. He doesn't close his eyes because behind his eyes he'll find me or else he'll find the Closetsong. He reaches up and strokes her rotten face.

"I don't believe you," he says.

She struggles free from me, suddenly moved. She whispers to him again though she knows that I can hear it, knows she will be punished.

"Good."

Her body goes limp and stiff, falls on top of him, his gaze locked with her dead face. He is trying not to cry or doubt his sanity. He just cries, lying underneath Antonia's body, a body which fades from view as he throws arms around it. Though dead, he can't help but treasure her as I do. I will have him, it will be so. I will beat him to death with history.

# MADDY AND CLARENCE AND THE FIRST GIRL

Maddy and Clarence are sitting at dinner. I don't know what moves me to give them this moment. It might be that I start to fear insubordination. Maddy was younger, much thinner back then. Her face had been softer, her eyes less wide and crazy. She thought back then they were happy together. She thought nothing of the times that Clarence made her wear a bag over her head when they made love, when he would make her call him "daddy" or play dead. She had thought back then that he was just stressed out at work when he would break a dish to make a point.

This was a man who loved her. He was handsome and a doctor. He was rich. She was proud to be loved by him even if she wasn't. She remembers this time as a time when everything was good, this time before The Kitten. Though I have shown her the times he treated his patients like he'd treated Kaz up in the study, she would not watch I made her watch and yet she would not watch. I could keep her in that room forever and she would never never take in that it was bad before The Kitten.

But this night when they are sitting at dinner, they are at their happiest. It might be so. How happy could they have been? They are enjoying a pot roast together, the fruit of an afternoon's labor. Maddy is the perfect housewife and Clarence the perfect husband, coming home from the office to a dinner wrought from an afternoon slaving over a hot stove.

"This is good," he says, straining. It is in fact a delicious pot roast but he is straining to tell her, to seem civil and not hate her for the weight gain and the children she can't have. Not that he would want to raise anything that came out of her body. He is trying to be civil because there's something he wants from her.

104

"Thank you. It's my grandmother's recipe." She doesn't expect him to want to talk about pot roast for very long and wouldn't want to go on for much longer and provoke his anger, anger he'd bring out in bed with something awful. So, she doesn't expect him to talk about pot roast very long. He is going to talk about something else now.

"I think I feel ready. To try this. Do you feel ready?"

"I thought you were joking at first," she says, lighting a cigarette, "I couldn't have imagined that you'd..."

Clarence stands up, puts an arm around Maddy's waist and draws her close. He speaks to her quietly, warmly, smoothly. He speaks to her essentially in his doctor voice.

"Very serious, Maddy. I think this is who I am. I promised, Maddy, that I'd never judge you for who you are. And I know that you would never judge me for who I am. I have needs, Maddy. And dreams. I have to be able to do this without feeling afraid. I have to do this and know that you still love me and approve of me for who I am. Do you love me, Maddy? Do you approve of who I am?"

She raises a hand to stroke his cheek.

"Of course I do, Clarence. I would never judge you. I love you."

"So are you ready for this, Maddy? Are you going to help me?"

Tears are pooling in her eyes. She is genuinely afraid. He didn't know he was this man before they came together and now she is scared that she knows who this man is and she approves of everything about him, even this, even the worst thing, even the thing that maybe would have made her say no to him. But this thing doesn't make her say no to him. His arm is around her waist, she's clutched close and she's safe.

"Yes, Clarence. I guess I'm ready. I told you I love you and I want you to be happy. If this is what you need to do..."

He shakes his head.

"No, Maddy. I just need to know. Just once. I have to see

if it feels right. I can never help but wonder."

"Would you like another helping of pot roast?"

Clarence would not like another helping of fucking pot roast.

"You're changing the subject."

Maddy nods.

"I am. This is uncomfortable. I didn't know this about you when we first got together. I'm not sure I would have… .I'm sorry for saying this."

Clarence hangs his head. He plays up the torture in him, he plays up the forces fighting for control as if it had ever been a fair fight, which it never was. The homeless girl he tossed into the Charles, throat slit, asshole caked with blood, appears in his mind's eye and he remembers the sensation of power, control and certainty that brought him and the knowledge that he could do it again and get away with it because he was smart and charming and respectable and clever, most of all clever. He lets the feeling of torture appear on his face while inside there is the ecstasy of knowing somebody will know what he's done and not only know but help him and not only help him but live day in, day out with the knowledge that they are a part of it.

"You shouldn't be. This isn't something regular people think. It's not healthy, no matter what I tell you. I have problems. I have a dark side, Maddy and I can't pretend I don't. I can't expect you to love me, not when I'm this horrible thing that I am. I can't deal with this alone and I need you to help me and make sure that I get through this okay. But I can't make you do that."

She holds his hand. She looks deep into his eyes, seeing the torment and crocodile tears he wants to project and the fear of disapproval that he wants her to think plagues him and the repulsion and the sick novelty of it. She looks deep into his eyes and she sees exactly what he wants her to see because he's good at that and that's why I need him and also why I brought them both back here. It is, in a way, two people renewing their wedding vows, not the starched white false vows they made before the imaginary deity that lurks outside my threshold but before the true god in their walls and in their lives.

"I'm here for you and if you need this, I'm here to help you. Til death do us part, I said and I've gotta take that serious. You need to know what this is like and if you can live without it."

He got away with this twice before. Twice before even meeting Maddy. He knew what it felt like already and didn't want to live without it. Clarence needed power and dominion over the wills of those around him. Clarence needed to be able to change hearts. Doing this just with patients and fucking just his patients hadn't been nearly enough.

"Thank you. I love you so much."

"I love you."

And then suddenly Clarence is out and part of the night that he belongs in. He is stalking and waiting and dreaming. It has been too long for him since the last time. He feels as if five minutes was too long. He wants to take everything with legs and tits back to his house, have his fill of it and finish it off while his wife watches. But he does of course pick one, hard as it is, he finds her, young and wide-eyed and desperate and stupid.

And then suddenly the First Girl is listening to a dashing older man at a bar, telling her she seems sophisticated for her age. And they're talking about Eastern Philosophy and yoga and energetics and all of these things that Micah and Cytherea go in for. And they're talking about politics and youth culture. And he's listening to her as she brings up how apathetic her generation is and wonders where the dream of the beatniks and hippies has gone. He's quoting Ginsberg and she's asking him what he does for a living. And he tells her he's a therapist, interested in Jung and Reich and all of these new techniques. And he asks her if she wants to go back to his place and drink some wine and smoke some marijuana. And of course she trusts him and wants to go back to his place and drink some wine and smoke some marijuana. He has always been good at making people trust him.

And she goes to his office in the study through the back door. He talks about not wanting to wake his wife and she giggles. It's an adventure. A dirty, secret adventure. She's never done it with a married man before. She whispers that she's a little ashamed of herself. He doesn't go in for shame. An antiquated Judeochristian concept that society would be better off without. Denying one's urges destroys the heart and soul.

They kiss. He touches her thigh. Her top comes off. Her breasts are big and conical and she isn't wearing a bra. She smiles at him and he smiles at her. Soon, they're naked together. Soon he's making use of her, not with the enthusiasm he'd use Antonia with. He pounds away at her apathetically, not like he wants to be pounding away at her, not in the way that I want him to either.

He suddenly pulls out of her.

"Hold on," he says, "close your eyes. I'm going to get something."

She closes her eyes, expecting handcuffs, expecting a blindfold. She does not expect a syringe full of tranquilizers to be pulled out of his desk. She doesn't expect to get dizzy, doesn't expect to hit the floor. And she doesn't expect that he'll keep going when she does. She doesn't expect a trembling, crying wife to come in and watch because he needs her to watch.

"I brought the hammer like you wanted," she says.

"You're going to watch, right?" he asks, urgent, momentarily ceasing his fuck.

Maddy nods, head heavy, invisibly anvilled. She doesn't want to see this. She doesn't want to think about the thing she married. But she watches him entering her again. She's surprised at how it feels.

It is exciting to see her husband so much in charge. It is exciting to see her husband punishing this little whore for being stupid and for trying to take him away. Her husband has become an instrument of justice, righteousness and hope. Manly, assertive and in the right, he fills her with a burning desire for him. She is shocked to witness the spectacle of him brutalizing this unconscious woman with his cock and feeling aroused by it. Her hand wanders between her legs and finds herself getting wet.

And then she squirms awake. Her panties are stuffed in her mouth. The man she had gone home with and chosen as a lover is tossing her around like a ragdoll full of meat. A woman is sitting in the corner of the room masturbating. She tries to pull herself away from him but the drugs have made her drowsy. He hits her with the hammer and a trickle of blood appears on her head, as if he had hit her just to chisel it out.

The hammer comes down again. He thrusts a few times. The hammer comes down again. She is pleading silently, though her mouth is sewn shut she is silently pleading. Maddy's hand trembles. She's not sure she could do this. She has never hit somebody before. Clarence's fucking gets more intense, her body is shaking from him. Her eyes are full of tears, her mouth is full of semen and her insides full of him. Maddy is mad. She might be mad at Clarence for betraying her but she finds herself madder at this dirty little whore for enticing him. She punches the First Girl in the stomach. And then again. Clarence strikes her on the head once more with the hammer.

She squirms. She bleeds. Bruise. Blood. Crack. Crack. Crack. Numbness. Less squirming. Clarence explodes with excitement. Maddy explodes with excitement. He goes at her fiercing, interspersing thrust and thrust with beating. Maddy cries out as the girl stops squirming. Seeing only red, feeling only cunt, he fucks her until he's good and empty, he fucks her until he can do nothing but collapse into his wife's arms.

And this, for Maddy was love.

# HEAP

I shouldn't trust the foe but I let it drag me along if only because I am confident in my godhood in this place. Kaz is bringing home junkies and Leah is eating buttons and Micah and Cytherea are entangled in coitus that neither one quite likes or comprehends. I should be paying attention to them instead but no, now it's this. It shows me a boy. I know who he is. There is only person he can be. I know what should be mine but isn't yet. I know when I'm being challenged or being taunted. Yet I go where it takes me.

The boy is sitting at a kitchen table. There's an older man with him, same hair, same eyes, same hunched and vanquished posture. The man's beard is a deep, dark wolfhaunted forest, shaggy and wild, a place where he conceals his heart from his child. Though this is a face Brian might one day grow into, it is also one that does nothing to betray its sentiments. There are four empty beers on the table. And a fifth one is open and in his hand.

"Did I tell you about the time I had to take a guy's eye out?"

Even if Brian had known, it looks like he would shake his head "no" and that there would be consequences if he'd said he had. So Brian of course shakes his head no because he is so small and this man so thoroughly drunk. He does not look like he wants to know about how to take a man's eye out or what circumstance it had happened in. But he is going to hear the story again, or just a fragment of it.

"Jarhead back then. It was during the swim test. You know what a jarhead is?"

Brian does not speak or move. He does not dare to say

"yes" or say "what it is" or that the father has told him the tale before. It takes herculean strength to make the move that he can make, the one move he can make. A simple nod but there might as well be an anvil at the end of the child's neck. The boy nods yes because that's what will get the story to the end without the flaming seraph sword of fatherly judgment falling down upon him.

"Smart kid," says Brian's father, ruffling the child's hair, "I was a jarhead back then. Taking the swimtest. But there was this guy there, an old guy in the pool. He'd done a couple tours in Vietnam, this guy. And he didn't come all the way home. I never saw action but there were some guys that never came all the way home. This was one of those guys, this guy."

This is where Brian knows that he's to speak. He must be fascinated. If he isn't fascinated, there's consequences. One of few things I could see about him is that he knows this game. This game is an important one because it's clear he's lost it before. I hope The Closetsong shows me its forfeits.

"So what happened?"

Something appears behind the father, a heap of shadows, a shadowy heap. It emits a stench like long neglected compost. Oh, is that what you smell like,? That's darling. It makes a sound like tiny hammers on pipes in the basement. So many tiny hammers. The father squints and folds his brow in pain. He tries to massage his temples but there are hundreds of secret hammers playing behind him on the pipes. Brian blinks again and again, trying to make the heap behind his father disappear or to see for real that it was never there.

The Heap is there. The Heap is actually there. And the hammers are getting louder, the compost is putrefying. And the father's eyes are starting to back away from the son, from the room and from the present. History catches and collars him, history manacles his wrists and brands his back. History drags him away.

"This guy started to think that he was somewhere, back

in Nam, maybe drowning in the swamp but he grabbed my
waist and started to panic and struggle, started to drag me
under, the more I fought, the harder he struggled against me,
the more desperate he was to drag me under the water with
him. I was going to drown. I was sure that I was going to
drown. But you can't panic. You need to learn to stay still
and quiet and think. I stop struggling and I moved quick.
You know what I did?"

Considering the theme and nature of the story, it is of
course clear what he did. There was only one thing that he
could do.

"I gouged the guy's eye clean out. That's what it took to
get him to loosen his grip. And then I swam away."

"Wow."

"That's why it's important that you learn to keep your
cool and be calm and quiet."

"Yes, dad," says Brian.

"There is nothing more important in life than to learn to
sit still and be quiet."

A child Brian reaches into an almost empty satchel of
words.

"Yes, dad."

The father reaches for the last beer in the six-pack and
cracks it open. The Heap is making a noise like the last
squeals of a dozen different animals. Brian is trying to get
up and explain why he needs to get up. The game is about
to change. His father has an idea. He doesn't like when his
father thinks he is improvising or can teach an important
lesson. His father's ideas aren't often good. This is going to
be a really bad one.

"Let's see how good you are at being still and quiet. Let's
see how you can hide."

"I...I want to go read a book."

The father takes a mighty swig of this last beer. He glares
at Brian.

"This is important."

There can certainly be no denying that this is important. The Heap has thoroughly made its presence known. It makes its influence so crystal clear. Do I look like that to Brian? Can he see me? What if he sees me, what if he feels my hand on all of this? What if he felt my hand in Antonia?

"Brian, I know you don't give a shit about being tough like your old man was. I know you're not a soldier, you're a sensitive faggot artist. Well, sensitive faggot artists gotta be tough."

Brian cocks his head, speaks up, even though he is certain that the room is ruled by the Heap and the consequence of questions might be disastrous.

"What's a faggot, dad?"

His father laughs, a braying, strange, not quite person laugh that comes from the tendrils of Heap, rubbing his shoulder, affectionately stroking his face and maybe soaking poison through his skin. The kid's funny, he seems to think. I don't get what's so funny. I am focused on the Heap and what it's doing and how it seems to be making them feel. He ruffles the boy's hair.

"That a boy."

Brian doesn't dare to ask again or to ask anything or to go off and read a book or put some headphones and a record on. Those things could lead to disaster and the situation is already balanced at the edge of a precipice of hellscape. It lurks in a cottage built teetering on a chasm and it can tumble and burst apart and all inside would also burst apart. He does nothing but await instructions. His father doesn't quite appreciate how much soldier he's actually put into the boy. He should. Good work has been done. Sad work but good.

"We're going to play a game now."

He pops open the last beer. Brian swallows. He really doesn't want to play a game.

113

"This game is about being quiet and still and keeping safe. I love you, son and I want you to be able to keep safe."

"Thanks, dad."

"You know how to play hide and seek, right?"

Brian nods.

"Yup. You hide and I count and then I find you."

The man shakes his head solemnly.

"No, son, not this time. You hide this time."

Brian shudders a little. His voice cracks a bit as he forces a phrase from his mouth.

"What if you don't find me?"

Children are as stupid as they are fragile. So senselessly trusting, thinking that he's better off with this man around. The child knows so little about men. The child knows so little about what he lives with and about the influence of the Heap, the big black thing growing up to the ceiling. The rival wallsgod exerts its influence often. Throws its weight around almost bad as I do and is almost as heavy as I, almost as old and as angry and unstoppable as I.

The father smiles and the smile bites the boy.

"Well, that's the idea, Spook."

The man takes another swig of the beer and puts his hands on his eyes. He does not wait for the kid to say that he wants to play. There is no not playing this game. There is no winning it either. This is a game where one can but lose. These are the games I play and I play them well and I play them proud. It annoys me to see that the boy has played them before. What is one to do against a boy who has played these games before?

"One...two...three..."

Brian ascends the stairs, walks into his parents' bedroom, following a whisper, a seductive whisper from inside of the closet. He walks up to the door, opens it and steps inside. This mistake will follow him forever.

# IN THE ROOM

The door to the bedroom is gone. Micah and Cytherea end their evening's revelries and stand up, getting ready to wash up or to grab a drink of water but the door to the bedroom is gone. They examine the wall that once held the bedroom door, patting it down for signs of what's not there. But the bedroom door is gone, I have concealed it. And they are not getting out.

"It has to be here," says Micah.

"You mean you can't see it either?" asks Cytherea.

"No," he says, "I can't see it either."

They sit down on the bed, eyes closed, both trying to think. Both of them are trying to find the very very obvious idea that they have a bedroom door, which anybody's bedroom would have. Except for theirs. Except for this one. They had come through that very door not an hour earlier and now it was gone. They open their eyes again almost in tandem, almost as if it was always just one set of eyes. And once more they see their pagan tapestries, their collections of statues and icons in shallow commitment to Eastern religions that they have stolen bits and pieces of practice from, their framed prints of dragons but they do not see a door.

They sit in silence. They look back and forth and each other and at the wall. Was it the marijuana? The wine? Which was it? Was it the drugs or the drink walking on their brain? Micah walks to the wall and tries to open it like a door. It doesn't open because it's not a door. Maybe it was never a door. Maybe they could never escape this room. He sits back down on the bed.

"Something is fucking going on," he says, "there's

115

something fucked up going on around here lately and I don't know what it is."

They stare together at the wall and hope the door will manifest. They wonder together where it went, hand in hand, sighing, praying under their breath to the old gods they've adopted, the gods who don't matter in these walls. He asks Pan, he asks the shape I took used to take him in his dreams to set him free from these delusions. They close their eyes again then open them once more to find a wall instead of a door. The First Girl smells starvation so blinks in almost as if to tell them "as you are so once was I." Then blinks back out, though she will be brought back in.

"Maybe," says Micah, "maybe we've been dosed."

Cytherea thinks back to the events of the day, what they've consumed and where they went. They hadn't really been anywhere or eaten or drank anything strange. They hadn't gotten into their own stash of drugs beyond smoking a bit. She examines events and finds that indeed, there could be nothing alien in their system. If there is nothing alien and nothing alien in their consciousness, then indeed they must be in a room with no door.

"We haven't been dosed. The door is gone."

Micah stands up. Pounds on the wall. Pounds again harder. Screams. I swallow the screams, soak them into the walls, muffle the sound of pounding. They are too much mine to change the walls I dwell in, they are too much mine to shout out of this room. He pounds until his fist bleeds, soaking a drop of blood into the wall that I soak in, almost just to show him that I can do that.

"Why? Why is it gone?"

He smashes the wall again again again as if he has the might in his body to cave it down as if his rage makes him larger and tougher and turns his fists into anvils of hurt that will make dust and drywall rain down and the palace come down around him completely.

# INVESTIGATION

Brian trembles as he climbs the stairs. He has given enough to me that I can see bits and pieces of his reasonings. He wants to see that there is nobody in the study. He wants to know that everyone around him is going nuts because he suspects that everyone around him has gone nuts. Nobody has seen or spoken to Kaz's doctor before. He comes in quietly through the back and sits down in the study and they meet and they can hear crying and moaning sometimes. None of anyone's business though it's certainly not right for Kaz to keep fucking her doctor. What the fuck kind of doctor is this?

Brian had a key made it seems. I couldn't follow him out so I didn't know this. He knows this is the day when Kaz has her sessions. He is trembling as he climbs the stairs because he's afraid of throwing open the door and finding Kaz in there speaking to an actual doctor. He's trembling because he knows that when he throws open the door, this is not what he'll find. He stops two steps from the top and he sits down. He looks like he's contemplating prayer, as if his prayers could penetrate these walls and reach a god that resided somewhere outside them instead of the one with them who is the only one that can listen. Which is, of course, me.

The Closetsong drifts him back, taking him for a moment to the man in the grey suit and to the great black Heap that stood behind his father before his father brought out the belt and taught him manners. He holds his shoulders and shivers. This is an icy chill, a chill of terror and one of realization. Were haunted houses simply haunted houses or was his life itself every bit as haunted? He thinks the word "ghosts" dozens and dozens of times. He looks down the stairs, which I take time

117

to contort, which I take time to enlarge in his mind, to make him childsized and smaller once again.

He can turn the key or he can go back downstairs. He can hear a voice talking softly behind the door and he can see the chance of freedom and the chance of escape yawning wide underneath him, a great chasm of possible cowardices seeking to absorb him. I do not know if I want him to open the door or flee. This is a tough decision. I'm sure he'll make the wrong one, though. It is in people's natures.

He climbs the stairs. He goes to the door and listens, hearing Kaz crying.

"I don't know who it belongs to. I just don't know. And I'm scared. It's growing in me and it's getting bigger and it's angry to be in there. It's scared and angry to be born. And I don't blame it. What kind of mother am I going to be? How can I raise a child. I'm not stable enough. I'm not sane enough to raise somebody's child!"

He tries to quietly let himself slump down but her words are devastating, a low and crushing blow that leaves him folded on the ground. He crosses his arm against his chest and tries his hardest not to cry. It could be his. They did what they did when they did. The time would be right for it to be his. And somehow she doesn't even remember. Ghosts. We're being fucked with. Something in this house is fucking with us. Something is fucking with us.

"I think I should get rid of it. I keep hearing this voice in my head that tells me to get rid of it. I'm not ready for this. I'm not somebody's mother. Yeah, I think I'm going to get rid of this thing. I don't even know who the father is. That's how unstable my life is right now."

There is silence. He doesn't hear anybody talking back. Kaz is talking about a pregnancy she doesn't remember with a doctor that isn't there. He walks away. He knocks on Micah's door. They haven't talked much, him and Micah. Micah's always working out or spending time with Cytherea or fucking Cytherea or fucking someone. Micah has his own world. Not like Kaz or Leah or Brian. Maybe Micah won't be worried about Kaz at all. Something is fucked up though and something is fucking with everyone. Micah believes in New Age shit. Maybe Micah believes in ghosts, even though Brian doesn't quite believe in ghosts.

Micah might believe in ghosts but he is occupied. Cytherea and him are curled up in an urgent embrace, tears in eyes. Please please please let this end. Please please please let us find the door. Please please please out. Please out. Please. Please. Please let the walls let the walls be thin again, please let them break right down. Please let us out. Please let us be heard, please let someone come in so it isn't just us alone in the dark with the knowledge that there's nothing else in the world. Please let them smell the stink of our shit as it piles in the corner please let them care its there. Please let them let us out. Please let us out.

"Micah," says Brian.

"You there?"

"Cytherea?"

He knocks again. I let them hear the knock. I let them know there's something and someone else on the other side of the wall. They wish that he could hear them but he'll never hear them again.

"He's out there," says Micah, "the house is still out there. We haven't been sent somewhere else."

Cytherea gets up and listens at the wall. She hears the knocking on the door that is supposed to be there and the sound of a roommate shouting in concern. A roommate who hasn't seen them for two days, two days that they believe might have been a year. For them it has been longer. For awhile, they had retreated to separate corners of the room. Cytherea has read a couple books. Micah has read a couple books. They have each turned on their computers and found the internet out. They have found their phones get no signal.

When you have faith in these walls, I am God.

Brian tries one more time.

"Hey, Micah? If you've got a sec, I'd like to talk you about something."

"Brian!" Micah shouts out, "We can't get out of here! The door is gone. I don't know why but the door is gone. How long have we been in here? It feels like forever."

Brian listens at the door that is not there to them. He cannot hear any activity coming from inside. He can't hear the words being shouted out and directed right at him. He doesn't know they've been trapped there and what that means. He thinks he is simply dealing with a ghost. He decides that they are probably just out. They are probably just out somewhere, that's it. He moves on, still unnerved over Kaz and seeking some sort of companionship and contact or at least someone to tell what has gone down.

So, he of course goes to the door of his remaining roommate. Leah has not been out in a couple days either. She has been looking thin and pale and acting a little weird. He has not seen her eat or socialize since the night when they all had Kaz's vodka together. He's been a bit concerned for her and would be more concerned if it wasn't for the fact that he had had sex with Kaz before and had had sex with a ghost in this very house. Leah's behavior would have been disturbing had it not been in the context of all these other tragedies and absurdities.

Leah's behavior has therefore mostly gone ignored. Ignored of course unto the point of death. He knocks on her door unsteadily, slowly. He doesn't even really know if he wants to see her. He needs to see her, they need to talk about all that has gone on but he is still not sure that he actually wants to. She doesn't respond at first. I don't let her. I reach into him a little and try to tell him to keep on walking but he doesn't take my suggestion. He doesn't have to take my suggestion every time, he isn't mine enough yet.

So I let Leah come to the door and open it.

"What is it?" she asks.

"I need to talk to you about Kaz," Brian begins.

Leah closes the door and locks it.

"Leah, this is important," he says, "Leah, something is going on. Something really fucking weird is going on."

She doesn't respond. I don't let her. I want him to think that he's been locked out and simply could never count on her. I want him to think he is surrounded by hostility. I want him to think about calling the landlord, a call that will drop as he tries to get to him. What in the fuck is what this house? What in the fuck is with these people? I have to get out of here. I can't get out of here I can't I can't…

The Closetsong deserves some credit that's for sure. It beat this man into a fighter. I didn't see him for one. Scraggly musician made out of doubt. Sitting in the basement staring at the guitar he's afraid to play. Fading into the arms of a dead girl and begging for her to stay. He wants her to stay so badly. He wants her not to be there. Because if she's there, she's dead and what then? There is a solution to this in acquiescing. It could be easy for him if he surrenders.

He flees from all of this nonsense into the basement. Why does he flee into the basement? Oh, delight. He is fleeing into her phantom arms and he doesn't know it. He comes down here for respite from this insanity. I can't spare him. I can't spare any of them. I don't even wish that I could. They're better off belonging to me. I'm better off with them. I don't care how well off they are. I don't care about them. I'll just have them. I have things. He sits down and he stares at the corner and then at the guitar.

"I fucked up," he says to the guitar, "I should have stayed. We had a good thing going."

He looks around the room and sees that nobody is there and he keeps talking. At least he doesn't think there's a doctor here. It's okay to talk to yourself if you think nobody is listening. He's out of beer and doesn't want to buy anymore. He doesn't want to buy another dimebag off of Micah. He just wants some peace. He wants to stop feeling like he's alone. Like he's not alone. And to know that in both he is right.

"I…I was scared you'd go. And that I'd end up someplace like this. And I'd be sitting in a basement full of gear staring at a guitar. And here I am. I'm sorry. I should have stayed."

I can see that he had been afraid of something. Contaminating her and spreading the Closetsong. I can understand that. It's a nuisance and a pestilence. It's ruining my home. It's ruining those who are mine. He knew it was in his blood and in his bones and caked on his flesh and if he got too close then he would cover her in it and it would clump together and cluster and ooze and eat her and he would be alone again sitting in some dark basement again, staring at the guitar and not playing it and waiting for something or someone who wouldn't come or even if they'd come they wouldn't come.

He prepares to stand up and pick up the guitar and see if maybe he can still play it. She liked it when he played it. Said he had promise with it. Wondered why he never did. Wondered why he didn't like to sing. He sang to her and played it a lot. And now, here it is in one of the corners of the room, facing the one where Antonia's cage once was. The basement is a place for neglected things. Brian seems to put himself in this category. From what I've seen, it's altogether justified for him to do so.

Maybe he will give me some gratitude. Maybe he will open himself all the way and listen to what I think is best for him. Maybe he'll become mine altogether if I give him something he wants. I do it for the others and in spite of his mad inscrutability, he does deserve the same. I can be a courteous god. I can be a loving god. So, I extend him some courtesy and love and remind him what I have for him.

She shimmers into sight as if reality itself were a curtain

she hid behind. And she opens the curtain and reveals that she is here. She approaches him at his mixing chair and puts two hands on his shoulders. She sits down. He doesn't want me in but he's consented to touch her and doesn't see the connection because he's far too short sighted for all of that. She looks him in his beleaguered eyes and she sees the Closetsong and whoever he is pining for in them. And she knows that whoever he is longing for, it's her.

"I'm sorry you're hurting today," she says.

"I'm doing better than you are," he grumbles, gravel and acid.

"You're in pain so I'm going to pretend you didn't say that."

She kisses him on the cheek, rubs his warm face with her cold and lost one. He closes his eyes and lets her because it feels better than where he was and feels a whole shitload better than the rest of this day had. He lets himself go and wraps two hands around her almost nonexistent waist. He seems to know he's holding onto nothing but he holds it no less tightly. He knows he's all fucked up like that. They're quiet like this for awhile.

"You're not real," he says, "you're a dream. Or you're dead."

She cups his chin in her hands. She struggles hard against the tethers I have on her. She practically growls at him. She practically bites him. She practically walks away and none of these things would be worse for him than any other. And none of these things would be worse for her than any other. She thinks a moment and sighs. She leans in and she actually does bite him.

"Ow!" he backs away, then doesn't push her off at all.

"I want you to remember that I did that and that I can. Don't you ever tell me I'm not real. I'm right here."

"I'm sorry, I don't know how this works."

"Does anyone?"

There is silence again, filled with the possibility of being thrust back into old damnations and the thundering hungry void that is being alone. There is silence again and the prospect of the Closetsong or the cage or anything like it. But I don't rip them away from each other. Not yet. I have to see this. I have to know what she does when I don't pull on those strings. I have to know what she's learned from watching him and how it's made her feel about him.

"Can I kiss you?" he asks.

"You've done it before," she says with a shrug.

"Then it happened."

She winds up to bite him again but stops herself. Antonia is more frustrated than Antonia. She has seen and been through too much and knows too much of love like Julie did. She struggles to straighten up and be a patient person and show him the love he's called on her to show him. I must admit her treasure her strength. I must admit that some things and people are better to have than others and that this one in particular is terribly precious to me. I hate when I am forced to be sentimental but it is so.

"Yes. It all happened. I am dead but we held each other and we kissed and we made love. And I liked it. I promise."

He sits and digests her words, words he has known had to be true. He held her. He knows the taste of her skin and her mouth and her body. He knows what it felt like to hold her even as she rotted away. There can be no more deceiving himself. There can be no more attempts to forget. There will be no more forgetting. He sighs. He buries his face in her shoulder.

"Then are you going to disappear again?"

"I'm dead," she says, "I don't know what to tell you. Can't you just enjoy this? Do you have to question? Do you have to be afraid?"

"But you're dead."

She kisses him quickly. He wishes she hadn't. But still,

he kisses her. He tells himself that she won't fade. He tells himself that this is real and not going away. He tells himself it doesn't matter if she does. He lies with all his might. He kisses her and that's true but everything in his head at the moment is a lie. He kisses her and looks at her expectantly. And again they are quiet and just enjoying their warmth and again they are waiting for pain or disaster to come and wrench them away.

I don't take her. I don't tell her I'm going to take her. This is about watching. This is about seeing if they'll console each other and seeing if she actually wants what she wants. She breaks the silence with another kiss, full of force and fervor made to anchor her to there and then. They keep in the there and then, they keep next to each other, quiet, save the kisses and the sighs, quiet save urgency.

I listen to them swallow. I listen to them waiting for me. I listen to them knowing that they are at my mercy even when he doesn't know at all what it is that I do and am. They clasp hands in their quiet agony. They stare into each other's eyes again in their quiet agony. He tries to breathe out words that keep getting choked back, she tries to tell him not to speak, not to touch her, the reason he shouldn't speak or touch her. The tethers, the tethers feel so thin on her right now.

Is she mine? Will she stay mine? Why is she mine? I am trying to search her for answers but she somehow feels far away. This makes me mad. I hear it in him and through him in her the sound of that pounding on pipe. I know it is in her, the Closetsong because if it is in him, then it's in her right now. They are sharing this space and this world they're building between them. I can feel him close enough that I can see he is afraid of her being taken away.

And yet he expects for her to be taken away or for her to go herself. He makes it hard for me to do this to him. Does he think it inevitable that she'll be torn away? He's waiting for me to do that. It will be hard to hurt him then.

Do you know that you're praying? You've never prayed

125

before. Do you know that you are on your knees before the sacred icon that is me? Do you know that you are praying? Because you are. In these walls, I am god. And I am worse than god. You are on my knees before me because you long. The sighs and tears that long to escape that long to call for her are calling for me. Do you know that you are on your knees and waiting for my response? Would you ask me to make it rain from the ceiling? Would you ask me to help your crops grow tall? Would you ask me to smite your enemies? Because if you ask me hard enough, I will.

We are not enemies, you and I. You need not be my foe. Nobody needs to be my foe, since all men who cross this threshold are mine in the end. The time you spend opposing me is time spent harming yourself. The time you spend opposing me is time you spend without. Why spend time without when you can have all that you long for? It is fortunate that you only long for one thing and that this thing is mine.

You're sitting there in this basement on your fifth beer of the night and you're staring at the corner as if the walls will shift and reveal behind them everything you've dreamt of. If that's something you want then I can do that. They're my walls after all, this is my temple. You're sitting in this basement on your fifth beer of the night and you are asking me to bring her as if you have done something for me lately to make me bring her.

But conversely, defiant boy, you are meditating on fingers and meditating on breath, you are listening for whispers of "yes, I'm with you" even though you have to know she isn't. How could she be with you if you're not with me? You could break that bottle right now and you could take the shards, yes, just take the shards and carve up. Not horizontal, vertical. Rise up into me, evaporate into the ceilings, evaporate into my heavens, evaporate, so you might rain down again and be part of this.

I can feel you considering it and understanding the

incentive I've provided. I've provided enough incentive. If there was God outside these walls, he hasn't given you that which I've provided. If there was God outside these walls, then you'd be petitioning him instead of me and your heart is petitioning me since you know I'm here and you cannot know if anything or anyone else is here. How do you even know she was ever here? How do you know she isn't just a silhouette projected on a wall for your amusement?

You think that I can't talk and walk and smell like a girl? You think that I can't make skeletons dance on puppet strings projected from the heavens? Do you really think I can't? You know better and that is why you're praying because I am the only one who can give you back what you want. What you want is so simple and so much mine. Come on out and ask me. Verbalize it. I WANT TO HEAR YOU ASK ME.

You're hesitant. Why? Because you don't trust me? Because you think I'll drag her away again like everything life presents you, steaming banquet that turns to dust on your tongue? That is the nature of having and the nature of want. I want you. I am going to get you. I am going to make you tell me you want to do whatever pleases me. You will cut the throats of everyone around you, as if it was necessary. You will drink their blood and call for me for whatever name I tell you is mine.

And that name will be a lie because I don't owe you the truth and you'll never get it. That's what you should know by now. You think you have a grasp on this and your ghost stories will serve you well. You think I'm just a cadaver like all the puppets. Come dig at the foundation deep as you can, deep as magma, deep as dinosaurs, dig down to the center of the Earth and you will not find my cadaver. It's not so easy. You will not pour holy water on my head and anoint me. I will be the one anointing you.

Brian has made me angry. This is what I'm telling him but he cannot quite hear it because he is not mine enough and I must tell him this because he is not mine enough. I do not like being mad. It gives them ground and it is giving ground to the Closetsong and the Closetsong's agenda. The Closetsong, the intruder, the other set of eyes on them takes pleasure in my anger. A Heap that rises up and engulfs the hearts around it, the Closetsong would have me engulfed in it too. But no more. At least he is praying. The Closetsong can't make him pray. I showed him something dear enough to pray for.

He does it. He says it aloud.

"Come back. Please, come back. I need you."

He needs those hands and smells and breath and words. He needs that body pressed to him to remind him that his still works and his heart still beats even though hers has not for so many years. I can give him her heartbeat and give her heartbeat. He's praying for it but I'm waiting. He needs to make this mistake. He needs to see just who he is dealing with.

"Come back, Antonia."

Antonia begs for me to let her come back. She tells me it's not fair to do this to her. I am inclined to toss her through time again, back to the moment of death and back to the cage and back to the time she spent in it. She knows how to pray and knows I can answer her prayers but I'm not at all happy that she would dare call me unfair. There is nobody as fair as me. The exchange is even. I have them and they have what they want, though most of what they want is dictated by me. The exchange might be uneven but it's fair because it's fair to me.

I send him her shadow on the wall. It flickers into being. He can see the curves and know that something casts it. He can see just what's not there to cast that shadow, just who's not there. He reaches out for it but stops himself, knowing its just a projection and she isn't solid. The Closetsong reminds her that she's dead and that he's strong enough for loss and that he's already lost so much. It tells him he should just succumb to it, go back to the moments he spent inside the closet, go back to the hell he knew instead of the one he doesn't.

128

"No."

The world seems to tremble with the weight of this word. There is so much potential in the weight of this single word. He's telling me I'm winning and that he'd rather choose to suffer something new. Very well. I would call that a prayer. It's not a bad one. I let the shadow reach out a hand and stroke his cheek. He knows it's just a shadow and that it's cold but he welcomes her touch because he knows that it belongs to her.

"Come back here, please, I need you. I don't know who took you away but you need to fight it."

She tries to mouth the words "I can't" but she is just a shadow and she belongs to me too much to slip away again. I'm not going to let her slip away again. The things I own are precious because I own them and I am committed to having. The playthings of gods are precious and make the toybox precious. And this one is more precious than the others. It's alright that I admit that. This one is precious and she belongs to me.

"Come back here!" he shouts. He looks like he feels like winding up and slapping her. She'd probably like it. She's been taught to like it. I'm tempted to give him her face for just a moment so he can feel his backhand making that fatal mistake. But something shakes me. Something makes me suddenly ill at ease. She is yanking on the strings, punishment or none, she is yanking on the strings, she's terribly solid. She reaches out beyond me and she does something I don't let her.

The shadow wraps its arms around him, makes itself flesh if only for a second, a second that I will punish her with decades for. I am surprised. She is so solid during this moment, ablaze with impertinence, fiercely his but beyond that, even worse than that, the worst thing that anyone can be in my sanctum, in my temple—she is fiercely and utterly hers. I cannot pull her away to punish her, something is stopping me, not just the Closetsong but the sudden, ferocious force of will that she is exhibiting.

"Come back to me!" I snarl at her.

"Let her stay," he says under his breath.

The Closetsong is shuddering. The Heap is getting small. It knows what's just happened. Antonia knows what's just happened and she gives her all to cling to that flesh and claim another moment just as he clings to the idea of her possessing that precious flesh and possessing herself. He has prayed to me now. He has called out to me specifically. So this time, I oblige him completely. I let him keep her in his lap because he asked me to. I let her keep his flesh because he asked me to. I let myself creep into his mind and spirit because he asked me to.

I glean so many secrets that the Closetsong didn't tell me. The Closetsong had that leverage over me but it doesn't have it anymore. Beaten by his father, tormented by the Closetsong, living his whole life in denial of what he saw, telling himself that building after building would be safe. Trying to take risks but afraid to really stick out because it was better to stay hidden and stay safe. Cursed by pills and liquor, a desire to numb and make it go away, giving the Closetsong so many opportunities for it to keep its promise.

He lost one girl he lost to drugs and infidelity. He tried to keep her from going out and scoring again and from bringing home men while he was at work. He begged her to stay healthy, begged her to go into the hospital but she never did because she loved her poison and her infidelity more than she loved him. She believed in him and the guitar. He never felt he held her tight enough. He had always thought that love would find a way. It never did. I see now why he is so fond of Kaz and yet he fears her so. She smelled familiar. They have a child together now but he doesn't know that yet.

The other girl he lost was more precious still. This one actually loved him and supported him. This one believed in him and his guitar and did her best for both him and the guitar. This one loved his playing and loved him. This one he could never tell the truth. This one didn't know what lurked in the closet and this one didn't know his doubt and his fear and his silence and what they meant. This one is the reason that he doesn't play the guitar. He lost her and all that he had to do to lose her was to be himself.

This is a man who loses again and again. He cannot do anything but. He can run and he can hide in the safest, darkest spots that he can find but he will always be found and he will always lose and life will bring down the belt again and I will bring down the belt. Antonia is mewling like a kitten. She is genuinely afraid and well she should be. She knows the price that he is choosing to pay and how he will end up paying it. She knew he would lose from the getgo but she does not want to be a part of it and doesn't want him to lose because of her.

"You shouldn't have done that," she says, as I peel flesh from her face to once again remind him that he makes his sacrifices for a dead girl like a fool and nothing he can do can let her live again. I peel the skin from off her chest and let him see the muscles and sinew and the ribcage and the beating heart. I let him see what he is giving all this up for and how funny it is to me that he would make this choice. And then I replace the muscles and then I replace the bones and then I let him see again the skin that identifies her as her and that the woman that he gives this up for is still there, she is still right there for him and that he should be grateful.

"You shouldn't have done that," she repeats, "he'll have you now and he can do whatever he wants with you. There will be no escaping him now no matter where you go and you'll be part of these walls just like I am."

"You're worth it," he says, which makes her hiss at him like a cat.

"Worth it for you the living to trade freedom for the dead? You goddamned fool, you really have no clue."

She holds him.

"I WAS MURDERED."

"I know."

"No," she says, through fog of tears and choked up sobs, "you don't and you couldn't possibly know just what that means and what it makes me. And what it's going to make you. I should go now and leave you alone. You should flee this house, if he isn't already in you so deep that it won't matter. He might have gotten in you and that means you can't flee. Julie couldn't flee and she's come back here. You're going to be like me and like her and like Leah."

He shakes his head.

"Leah's alive."

"No. She's killed herself and she belongs to him now. She belongs to the house and the walls and the god in the walls. She is dead. And Kaz is dead. You can get out of here before its too late but it might just be too late. Especially because of what you just did."

"I'm not going anywhere without you," he says, strong, hard and obstinate.

"You risk your life for one already dead. You couldn't possibly be any more stupid, could you? What if I told you I never really cared about you and everything I've done is because of this thing manipulating me and that I'm nothing but an empty puppet and I could never love a man like you? Hmm? What if I told you that."

He looks up at her, a smile creeping onto his face.

"Then you would be a liar."

She peels the very flesh from her face again and from her breast and lets him see again that she is bone and viscera and no force of animation behind it. She lets him see for certain that she is dead.

"I need you to get out of here. There will be no end to our suffering if you don't."

"If he's murdered all of these people, then it's already too late."

She hangs her head. She knows that he is right.

"Then at least we will see a whole lot of each other."

# PARLOR GAMES

"Thank you for doing this," says Brian, "I feel like I'm fucking crazy."

"You are fucking crazy. But that's okay. I know the feeling."

A board game with a plank, a planchette is in his hand. He wants to speak to me with a children's toy. In a way, I suppose this makes sense, though he does not necessarily appreciate the irony of one of my playthings trying to treat me like I was just a game to be played. He sets the box down on the floor and replaces it with a beer, which he screws open quickly before handing Kaz a beer of her own.

"You sure we should be drinking and doing this?" Kaz asks.

Brian shakes his head.

"Fuck no," he replies, "there's no way in Hell we should be."

"I dig," says Kaz, taking a giant swig. She suddenly notices that Brian is very handsome. She remembers that she had wanted to have sex with Brian before all these things had happened with Doctorpuppet. Though she'd always wanted Doctorpuppet. She gets distracted by the thought of him inside her, those arms honed from playing and hauling gear pinning her down as he enters her. The game should bring them closer together.

She knows it's not just a game. She's seen the face of the First Girl and she knows that they're not alone here. She doesn't know how they aren't alone. She seems to think Doctorpuppet even has a home he goes to. She cannot possibly be this stupid. I see into her and know that she is not but that she would simply rather all these things make sense to her, terrible as they are.

They put their hands on the planchette, sweaty trembling hands that have touched and wandered across each other's bodies before though she doesn't remember. Their hands remember though, brush against each other, remember the architecture. Her hands hesitate some before they hit the planchette. She knows that this is wrong. It is very wrong.

"Hello," he says, "spirits in the house, we ask that you show your presence."

I bring forth a screaming Antonia, who shakes her head and tries so hard not to weep outright. She knows now to knock on the wall by her cage. She walks to the spot and gives the wall a rap. Kaz tries to pull away from the planchette but Brian covers her hand with his. He needs this.

"Sorry," Kaz whispers.

"It's okay," he says.

"Antonia?"

I shift the planchette to "NO".

"Is this the entity that haunts this house?"

I shift the planchette to "YES".

He breathes in. He closes his eyes. It takes a great deal of courage and energy to ask the next question.

"Where is Leah?"

I take great pleasure in this. He does not seem to know the depth and breadth of me. He seems to think I'm some little shit that spooks people and raps on walls and puts corpses behind him in the closet. He does not get that in these walls there lurks a god and that god requires sacrifice and restitution and that god must be honored with all his being.

"DEAD" I spell out.

Upstairs, I pull open the door to her room. I find myself hoping they will go up and check but they remain still. Kaz has had a sneaking suspicion that something is wrong with Leah and that suspicion was of course well founded. He sighs again, breathes deep again, if he prayed, he'd pray to something this time but he does not pray.

"Are Micah and Cytherea all right?"

"YES," I say through the planchette.

"They go out to things sometimes," says Kaz, "for a week or so at a time."

"They would have left a note," says Brian.

Kaz shakes her head.

"That's not what they're like."

And it isn't. They don't tend to show much concern or affection for those around them unless they want to use or fuck them. This is how the people around them could go for days without acknowledging they were gone and when they're gone all the way I can toss their bodies aside for as long as I need to.

"I'm worried," says Brian, "something's very wrong."

"It's nothing," says Kaz, "it's just a toy. There's nothing going on here. We should stop this."

Antonia moves the planchette to "NO." They will not stop, we will not tolerate it. He needs to know my sentiments. He needs to know just what he is dealing with. They both shudder. To have an unasked question answered is a disconcerting thing in a game like this one.

"What do you want?" he asks me. The question is large and laughable. What do I want? I couldn't answer it if I tried. All things that I see that can be had I have. So I want all things that can be had.

"LET ME IN," Antonia says through the planchette. He gulps. Kaz takes her hand off the planchette.

"I don't like this," we need to stop this.

"No!" Brian screams, "Something is wrong here. This house is haunted. This house is hell."

Kaz puts his hands on her thighs. She shakes her head "no."

"You're being crazy."

"Then what the hell are you afraid of?"

Kaz gets up and paces the room. She looks at the corner,

knowing what she's seen there, she lets her eyes wander to the stairs, which she considers running up. She wants to see if Leah is actually dead up there. But if she ascends the stairs she is confessing that something is wrong, that maybe her child and Doctorpuppet and everything in her life that is beautiful and good has been brought to her by something strange and terrible. So she returns to him and sits down across from him again.

"Fine," she says, face grim, "we'll find out."

"Will you show me what you are if I let you in?"

Antonia moves the planchette.

"Yes."

"Stop this," says the Closetsong.

He closes his eyes and concentrates. The Closetsong tries to push me away but he is begging to know about Antonia, he is begging to know about me. He calls out to me and I comply. I take him elsewhere. I show him things he does not want to see.

"Do you understand now?" I ask him, my voice reverberating through his body, through his mind and heart.

"This is my place. All who walk through this threshold belong to me and I may do with them as they please. I can give you this for one thousand years. I can drive them to destroy themselves and hide the bodies in corners of time and space where they will never be found. You must comply or she will see worse than this. You will call nobody. You will doubt nothing. You will stay here and you will take what you are given."

"I understand," he says.

"Do you get it?" I scream shrilly, "do you see?"

Clarence is pounding her ass and whipping her, nipples clamped, mouth gagged. Her shoulders shimmer with red and if I had a cock it would be three feet long right now. Her eyes are filled with tears and she is begging. She knows something is down there though does not know that something is me. She is unlubricated as always and blood is collecting. Brian's agape, Brian's trembling. Brian doesn't know what to do. Brian wants to help her, reaches out.

"STOP! STOP THAT!"

He coils back, lunges, punches Doctorpuppet in the back of his head. His fist goes clean through, a fist of the present that cannot touch a skull of the past. This does not stop him from screaming and trying more, which doesn't stop Doctorpuppet from fucking her ass some more and the gag doesn't stop Antonia from screaming more. This is history and history is a force of nature, bloodthirsty and implacable. History rapes and runs roughshod over all.

"Stop! You son of a bitch! Stop!"

"You have let her in and so in turn let me in. I have taken you here to show you."

Clarence stops after what must feel to Brian as long as it felt to Antonia, something I have made sure is so. Clarence dismounts and Maddy comes down the stairs with a chair. She sets in down in front of Antonia and removes the girl's gag.

"You're such a dirty little whore. You know that? Such a stupid, illbred, cockloving, filthy whore. God can't love you if you give into all your dirty little fantasies, you know. You know what Clarence says. These aren't healthy."

"I know," says Antonia, "I just want you both so badly all the time. It surges through me and poisons my mind and my loins. I'm sorry but I can't resist you. I pray for strength to want to be good but I can't be good and maybe I don't want to."

Brian is chilled to see a mind disassembled like this, to hear somebody say words that have been carved on her brain by somebody else's abuse and brainwashing.

"You want so many dirty and terrible things," says Maddy stroking Antonia's hair, "I don't know what to do with you. We all want you to be healthy and safe and to make it to Heaven. We want you to be in good enough shape emotionally and spiritually to leave. And we know you want that."

"Yes, mother, I want that," says Antonia.

"But the problem," says Maddy, "is that you don't. Your asshole is bleeding, Antonia. Good girls don't let boys do things like that to them. Good girls don't want that. And you're looking at my pussy now, Antonia."

Maddy spreads open the lips with her fingers, showing depths that nothing should want to crawl into, starting to ooze with cream so thick it could have come out of a cock it looks like.

"Do you want to be free of this?" I ask him, "I can liberate you from this if you give yourself to me. Will you do that?"

He shakes his head.

"I can't look away."

I don't understand this. Antonia, Clarence, Maddy, the First Girl and Julie all want to look away, all want to be removed from these situations. But he is standing firm, even as Maddy grabs Antonia by the hair and pushes her face into her, controlling her like a marionette by yanking. Her face is so close and so deep, it seems like she could drown or slip inside and never emerge again.

Clarence is sitting on the floor, his cock hardening once more. He's starting to masturbate to the sight of his pet eating his monstrous wife's big fat, pustulent cunt, drowning it, maybe never to come out again. Brian still locks eyes with this nightmare. Brian still stares head on.

Maddy pushes Antonia's face away.

"You had your fill?" she asks.

Antonia shakes her head.

"No mother," says Antonia.

Maddy slaps Antonia hard across the face.

"You're such a dumb little fucking whore. You're lucky we're here to take care of and feed you, you know that? Otherwise, there's no telling what would happen to a stupid little shit-for-brains whore like you."

Antonia nods emphatically.

"Yes, mother."

# FAMILY BONDING

Kaz has gone out and brought another man home. This time it was not at the behest of the Closetsong. I have something to show it today, something I hope that it will hold close and sacred and will never forget.

Kaz shoves the gaptoothed stranger against the door. She kisses him something savage, bloody, unhinged. She clamps down on his bottom lip, holding back her laughter. His face is old and sunken in though his mind and body might have been something younger. His eyes are on the verge of tears even before the bite. His hair is the texture of straw but so much thinner. His body is bony, his heart so often either fast or slow. I do not want this thing but it's been presented to me and I shall take it if I absolutely must. And I absolutely must because it has crossed my threshold. I let one of them go and I will not make the same mistake again. I still think that it was the Closetsong that did that. Even if it wasn't, I choose to blame the Closetsong.

"Slow down," says the man, choking back fear. He has never encountered this kind of aggression before. He knows he has reason to fear her for what she is becoming. It's almost as if he can feel that she doesn't belong to herself. It's almost as if he can feel that she belongs to me. I have been very active after all, so the air is thick with me and all I've done.

She doesn't slow down. The tempo of her kissing and stroking only increases, the aggression only increases. Her hand is between his legs and she is squeezing. He wants to get free. He can't get free. He does not want at all to get free. There is nothing on the other side of freedom and there is plenty to be had inside of her. I consider letting him see

Doctorpuppet manifesting around the corner, cock in hand watching as the mother of his spawn starts in on this man. I let Doctorpuppet do his business but this man is scared enough that he might not surrender right and I can't quite have him not surrender right.

He nervously and tenuously ventures a hand up to Kaz's breast and squeezes. Kaz gives him a wicked smile, a confident knowing one as she lets go of him and pulls his hand to take him down the hallway with all the roughness and all the abandon of a child dragging their teddy bear bouncing up and down stairs. He can only follow even though he still quite justifiably fears her. For all that drugs and drink and jail have taken from him, he is not altogether unaware of the dangerous thing he is dealing with and what she could mean.

Her ears perk up. She feels a shiver up her spine. It is the sound of an infant crying. Mama mama mama mama mama mama. She ignores it, choosing instead to focus on the lover she is dragging up the stairs. She wonders where the child is, if her boy will be in the room. She doesn't want her boy to see this. She will have to send him away. She wouldn't want him to grow up wrong.

She opens the door to her room and finds Julie and Antonia there, both of them naked. I reach into this man, suggestible and aroused and weakwilled as he is and I show him the prospect of what could be. It is almost an inquiry. "Do you believe there are two other beautiful women waiting for you?" Leah comes forward and joins, them undressed, and though her breasts are gone and nothing more than ragged meat, she is still beautiful in her way. As is the First Girl, faceless though she is.

"My friends are here," says Kaz, "would you like to play with my friends?"

"Yes," he says. He would like to. He doesn't understand what's going on but he doesn't need to. He's lived a life of slavery to appetite after appetite. Reality's grown flexible and anything that feels good, he will take it, even if it doesn't make any sense. Nothing makes sense to him anyway. He will take the gift he's offered, strange as it is. He opens his mind to touch and to the thought that he is not alone. He opens his mind to Julie tugging on his zipper and leading him down to the bed.

Then he opens his mind to Antonia's hair brushing against his neck and her hands undoing his shirt. Kaz bites on his nipple as so many men have done to hers and he would make a noise but he is far too excited by the possibilities Antonia and Julie exhibit. He is momentarily repulsed by the bleeding beauty behind him, the topless Leah bending down to kiss him on the mouth but he grows to accept her wounds as he accepts her lips and her tongue, he tells himself not to think about the blood. Whatever is being done here is right and loving, whatever is being done here serves his body.

He shakes with bliss as Julie, naked, strawberry blonde and puckish, wordlessly sits on his dick, turning her tattooed back to him and bending down to kiss Kaz's face while she bites him. Leah, not wanting to be ignored by the friend that I have so graciously given her back and brought her close to forever, runs her hands down Julie's sides. Antonia hungrily kisses the lowlife's throat.

This man fades into a fog of lust and bliss, so much so that the skullfaced First Girl sitting down beside him on the bed to watch does not deter him. He even puts a hand on her surprisingly smooth and not at all rotted thigh. I am generous to him because I need a quick surrender. I am generous to him because what follows won't be pleasant. Especially not for Kaz.

The homunculus comes shambling into the room. The fuckaddled ignoramous does not notice. The fuckaddled ignoramous is starting to come and considering himself blessed as Julie dismounts him and Antonia takes her place. Antonia is a better trained lover than Julie, though it is hardly

Julie's fault she was no slave. Julie's face is soon buried in Kaz's cunt, which Kaz lies on the bed to enjoy. Leah catches that Kaz might see the creature so soon changes positions, doing her part to prevent Kaz from seeing the aberration by sitting down on her face.

So Kaz doesn't see that suddenly, the great thick babyheaded member of the homunculus has forced its way into the man's mouth, drowning out screams and beginning to choke him, or that the scalpel fingers are running along the man's chest in a strange parody of the adult passion the hulking baby had witnessed. It is only when she hears the gagging sounds and the telltale squick of the mutation's cock sending its issue down the man's throat that Kaz begins to know something is wrong.

She tries to break away from Leah and Julie but she finds the two of them surprisingly strong, especially for such a wispy creature as Leah. Leah's weight is focused on Kaz's face, on forcing more cunt juice into the squirming girl's mouth, and Julie's hands holding her thighs still feel like a vicegrip. Her arms flail about as she tries to break away or get Leah off of her.

But she cannot stop the infant from cutting and cutting, from making new wet sounds as the blades plunge in, harder and thicker, smashing against bone, cutting strands of muscle, making contact with organ after organ, including the one between his legs, which has been gracefully vacated by Antonia. It isn't long before drowning in the seed in his mouth and cut up many times over, the man's life finally oozes out.

Leah and Julie dismount and with Antonia's help they force Kaz down to the bed, where the First Girl scoots over to sit beside her. Kaz looks at the dead drug addict beside her and lets out a scream, followed by another scream as she sees that the thing she created did it.

"That was bad," she tells the infant, "you shouldn't hurt

people like that. I don't know what we're going to do. Things are ruined, they're gonna find out about you."

"Don't worry," says the mouth on the baby head on the creature's cock, "we love you, mama, and we will keep you safe."

"This is murder," says Kaz, "this is murder."

The deformed infant responds by lowering itself onto its mother, going back to the place from whence it came, the infant head expanding her cunt and ramming up and down it. Kaz begs for help but the girls belong to me. She begs her baby but the baby does not want to stop and she shudders with pleasure in spite of herself because the connection and the penetration are too intense, she can't ignore this. She cries out both in ecstasy and self loathing, in despair and satisfaction.

She cries out "no" and in this she does mean "no" but she also means more. The baby can't help but comply, it wants only to please its mother and to be pleased. Kaz is crying, she wants this to end, Kaz is crying and she'll do anything to make it stop.

"Do you want this to be over?" says Leah, toying with Kaz's hair.

"Yes," says Kaz in tears, "I need for this to stop."

The infant gets off its mother and it cries out, finding comfort in the arms of Antonia.

"There, there," says Antonia, "it will be all right."

The baby nervously shambles its way to the bed and understands what must be done. With a quick and merciful slice of its scalpeled fingers, it slits its mother's throat, delivering her to me.

# STUCK

"We are going to die in here," says Cytherea.

"This is your fault," says Micah. He's uncertain how this is her fault but when two people are alone in a room with no door, it is one person's fault and it will very quickly start to look like the other one's. They will be back to comforting one another soon. This is the cycle, even when there was a door, this was the cycle. Without the door, it is simply more pronounced. There are no bars to grab a drink at, no other partners with warm, welcoming beds. There's only this bed. There's only one bottle of wine and that bottle has been empty. There's no more food. Cytherea's stash of candy and Micah's jerkies have been exhausted.

That which exists is inside the room and one of the things that exists is the fact that it has to be somebody else's fault and there are only two somebodies in the room.

"How is this my fault?" asks Cytherea, ready to fire back at him that he must have summoned this with his workings with the goat and his surrender to the dark, prehuman energies that lie in wait in The Emerald Necklace. She knows that it could only be the goat. She isn't altogether wrong. But she's wrong in thinking it was all his fault. She too is mine, given over to me by taking him in as he took me in. Given over by the need to please a man whose desires only got darker and darker with desires that only got darker and darker and crueler and crueler.

"Those witchcraft books. The Ouija board. The rituals. What you and Helen did. I know about what you and Helen did."

She suddenly feels very afraid of him. She should have been afraid of him before but now she's starting, now she's seeing what he's like with me in him. He's burning with something. He's burning with me and the things that I didn't need to put in him. She is looking around the room for a weapon. She could grab the staff he practices with or one of her knives but she'd have to move pretty fast to subdue him. She knows she couldn't move that fast or hit him that hard.

"That ritual didn't do this. I didn't call anything down on us. You need to calm down. You're scaring me."

"Oh," said Micah, "I'm scaring you!"

His voice and heat are rising fast. He starts to close in on her.

"We're trapped in here, no door and hearing voices and I'm starting to scare you. You should be fucking scared. All your witch shit and you can't do shit about this. We're trapped here and you can't do shit. I'm very very scared because we're going to starve and die. We're trapped."

"You're not trapped," says Doctorpuppet, appearing from nowhere.

Micah picks up his staff. He holds it up, threatening to strike.

"Who the fuck are you? Are you doing this?"

Doctorpuppet laughs. He holds up his hands and extends them in a "weapons down" gesture.

"Me? I'm a doctor. And no, I'm not the one doing this. And you really don't need to worry about the one doing this. It's not going to be a problem."

Micah sets down the staff. He sits down on the bed. He breathes and tries to "center himself." He isn't centered. There is no centering. At the heart of this place, there is only me. I am the center and he would do well to remember that. But he can't because he doesn't know it.

"I'm sorry. We've been in here for what feels like days."

Doctorpuppet nods.

"Well, my friend, your assessment is not incorrect. You have been trapped in this room for days. You've been shitting in the corner and you're about ready to kill each other. You're both very lucky that I came. This situation can be fixed."

Cytherea crawls toward him, sits up, presenting her pendulous breasts to him. She brings to bear the smoldering intensity of a gaze that has absorbed many men with its confidence. Even though Doctorpuppet has had better, he still meets her eyes and still focuses on her and what she has to say. She is, in her way, a very powerful woman.

"What can I do?" she asks him, "there has to be something."

The two of them are so warped and so much mine that they can still think of little but using each other's bodies, few solutions but fevered, desperate stupid fucking utterly disregarding everything that Micah is to her. This is what she knows of desperation; that it's the heat between her legs. So sick, so mine. He takes her breasts into his hand and kneads the nipples with his fingers. Maddy's caustic breath is hot upon his shoulders but he doesn't notice.

"This man just appeared from nowhere," Micah screams, "how fucked is your head?"

She shudders as she notices that she is indeed being touched by a stranger. She becomes vaguely aware again, free enough from sleepwalk to be afraid and to back away, to cover herself.

"What the fuck is going on? Who are you and how did you get here?"

"I'm a messenger," he says, "from what I guess you could see as God. I've seen the answers to the things that have left you feeling empty for so long and I've come to tell you how you can free yourself from being trapped in this place and in these circumstances. I was a doctor but then I saw the light and I'm free. I got what I needed and the thing you would call God will give you what you need if you trust me and you trust in its divine will. Can you do that? Can you trust yourselves to the will of the divine."

Micah nods.

"Brother, I am a righteous man. I listen to the Earth. I get what you're saying. We're ready."

I pull Doctorpuppet away. This is as much for me as for him. I am doing this for me, I am doing this against the Closetsong. I am doing this for the same reason I do many things I do: because I can. He is holding Antonia in his arms, standing over the bloated, stinking body of his wife, his bloated stinking wife. She has set the broken bottle down on the floor in front of them. She's crying.

"I had to do it. Even though she's my mother, I had to. God told me it was me or her, God said that if I didn't do it then she would come for me and she would come for you. She was going insane. She's been hearing voices. She was going to kill me, she was going to kill me..."

Antonia's syllables are drowned out completely by sobbing, all the cohesion, all the sense fades out completely. She looks up, eyes wet, mind suddenly becoming clearer, even as her speech becomes garbled. This was the man who had picked her up and drugged her. This was the man who had used her and beat her and whipped her, then gave her to his fat, monstrous, hideous wife. This was the man who had put her in a cage in his basement and only took her out to attend church with him and that fat, monstrous wife. This was the man that had put an end to the thing that used to be a woman that she saw sometimes, floating around the house. I show Doctorpuppet exactly what is on her mind.

I show Doctorpuppet that she has seen the First Girl and that she knows exactly what happened to her. She could kill him like she'd killed Maddy and she could walk away with impunity, the police knowing that she had been tortured and that the man she had to kill had been a multiple murderer and a rapist. She had nothing to fear from him now. Though Maddy is dead on the floor, she is also standing behind him now, whispering to him.

"There is only one thing you can do now. We're in trouble now. She's going to get away and she's going to let them know about everything you did. You can't let that happen now."

147

"Why?" he asks me, "Why did you bring me back here?"

It is not as if I ever answer him. It is not as if I have done it for more than to insure my position and to supplement his anguish. He is here and he is hearing himself and in himself and witnessing himself hear her, feeling himself holding Antonia again for this last time and picking up the shard of glass from the floor as she starts to wiggle free from his arm. And he feels himself stabbing her again in the stomach, as he holds her still by her hair.

He feels himself falling on her as she starts to go down and even though the pink carpet cushions the blow of her head being bashed hard against the floor, it still does not protect her from the repetition of the bashing or from the thrusts and stabs with the broken bottle he picked up, the bottle that had fucked his wife to death. Held by the hair, he beats the back of her head on the floor over and over and over and over and over and over and over and over again.

"You whore! You stupid fucking piece of shit cunt!" he screams at her, "Do you know what you did, you piece of shit cunt?"

She doesn't answer, the piece of shit cunt whore, bleeding and dead, skull cracked, blood soaking into the carpet, which slurps it up with a ravenous and eager hunger, with all the hunger in me, which is a mighty, mighty hunger. Her head wound is soon dried out, her gut wound is soon dried out.

"You ruined my family," he tells her as he unzips his pants and struggles to work his cock. It stays flaccid and weak in spite of his urgency. He begs it to get hard again, begs it to get back to the place where it can give and get pleasure. He doesn't seem to acknowledge that there are two corpses here or he is trying to get hard enough to fuck a girl he just killed or a wife that she had just killed.

He slaps her dead face again. He begs me to let him go back. He doesn't know why I've chosen to punish him. He takes her neck, her throat that has no breath to draw out from

A God of Hungry Walls

it and he throttles it even though there's no more life to take.
He wishes he could kill her again and again. Witnessing it,
he no longer wishes this but would rather have the opposite.

"I'm sorry," says the him that's witnessing, "I shouldn't
have...this was wrong."

He finally manages to coax his cock to life. He enters her,
hand still on her throat, sobbing and choking as he starts to
fuck his grief away, though his grief won't fuck away and he
won't be any less fucked. He doesn't know I have places to
hide the bodies. In these walls I am god and the dead belong
to me. I can put them where I please. He knows he has two
corpses on his hands and that he is mad and all he knew is
gone. He wanted to have children someday though he never
wanted to. It's funny now that he hears himself thinking he
had since now he has a child and it is what it is.

Maddy stands behind him sobbing and I let him hear it.

"I promise, I'll get to you next. I love you and I miss you
and I'm sorry."

"It's over," says Maddy.

"It's over," says Antonia.

He keeps on fucking the corpse, he keeps on throttling he
throat, he wants her to be silent, he wants Maddy to be silent,
he wants this to go away. Everything was so beautiful only
hours ago, why can't it be like it was hours ago.

"He can take back you there," says Antonia, "he can take
you back to when it was all right."

He pulls out, now understanding, now seeing that there is
nothing he can do, now seeing that the shard of glass is his only
way out. And with the shard, he decides to take this way out.

And then I bring him back to Cytherea and Micah.

"Break the bottle," says Doctorpuppet.

"Excuse me?" says Micah.

"Break the bottle," Doctorpuppet replies.

With a solemn nod, Micah does as he told and history
repeats itself again.

149

# NEVER STOP HURTING

I am playing with my entire toybox just to watch them dance. Doctorpuppet's ancient cock is pumping in and out of the holes in Leah's chest. Cytherea is licking shards of glass from Maddy's cunt filling the beastly old bat with a surge of surprise and delight. Julie and Micah are taking turns on the First Girl as the addict, flickering in and out of being, unable to touch the spectacle around them. Kaz is on the floor in a tempest of sensation brought to her by the aberration she's wrought. But I don't have them all.

Brian has the planchette again. He is seated on the pink carpet and staring into the corner, in the basement where the one he loved was lost.

"Do you want me?" he calls out to me, as if I would answer the question or as if he doesn't know. He punches the wall. Scrapes his fist, scrapes the drywall. He thinks he can agitate me by defiling my temple or that I am the temple itself. Both of these things are true but not true enough to serve him right now. Do I want him? Yes, I want him. He must be mine, his heart and soul and the Closetsong that sticks to him. He punches the wall again and again until his fist bleeds.

"Do you want me?" he shouts out, angry. Arrogant. He acts as if he doesn't belong to me already. He has prayed to me and begged me and made use of the things that are mine and lived inside these walls that are so much mine and he asks me if I want something that I have. I let him see the face of the First Girl again and then the big, sardonic smirk of Doctorpuppet.

I know he wants to punch the smile off of Doctorpuppet's

face. I know what he thinks of Doctorpuppet and that he would put an end to the man's life if he were still alive. I do not blame him. Antonia is precious to me as she is to him. He would not deserve to live. Inside my walls, possessed by me, nothing and nobody is living.

"You can have me," he says, "show me the way."

Doctorpuppet obliges him with a smile. He reaches into his pocket and pulls out one of his scalpels. Maddy emerges to play with herself and watch, giggling and tittering like a schoolgirl. Leah emerges, surgical masked, topless, exposing two open red crevices where once her breasts had been. Her ribs threaten to rip their way out of her skin. Her legs are sticks that shouldn't be able to hold her up. She pulls off the mask and throws up on the floor, a pile of buttons.

"CUT" they spell out.

Teetering on its awkward and broken body, the homunculus approaches. Kaz holds the monster up, tenderly planting a kiss on its oily red shoulders. It growls, recognizing Brian as a part of its grotesque genesis. The infant head on the edge of its grotesque, overinflated cock opens its mouth.

"Die now die now die now die now die now."

"You don't need to hurt me," he tells it, "I understand."

"No!" Antonia screams, "Fight this!"

Treasonous whore. I could take her away from this but then she wouldn't get to bear witness, she wouldn't see what she gets for loving him and wanting to be had by him. She is had by me and there can be no other having. He approaches Doctorpuppet and takes what he is offered.

He makes the first cut. Antonia looks into his eyes and begs him with her gaze to stop what he's doing, to somehow gather up whatever it is inside him that she's in love with, as if what she values in him makes him bigger than me, more important and capable of freeing this all from me. But he isn't. He cuts again and he opens himself to me, knowing that he has to surrender. And he cuts again and he starts to bleed and he gives himself to dying.

He fades and he draws into me, he starts to fade and starts becoming mine. He opens wide and I let in his thoughts, his dreams, his heart, the size of his love for Antonia, the weight of his longing, the regret and the abuse. I can taste every drink he's had and I can taste the need for the ones he hasn't yet. I can taste the fear and fervor and fever. I can taste it all and I know what it is to be him now and I know what it is to live with the banging of pipes and the sound of the Closetsong.

He had tried to ignore it for so long and forget it in the corners of his mind but there's no forgetting that clanging and there's no forgetting the Heap standing behind his father and the fear and confusing it engendered. There was no way that anyone could have forgotten, no way that anyone could have touched that without having to walk around with it forever. How has he endured that? How has he lived with the unbearable joyless noise and all it meant?

There is a strength that let that happen. There is a will. He's so quiet and so desperate because it was heavy because day in and day out, most of him was devoted to living with it. This haunting has come with him and it is a part of him. I see that blackness in him and as he comes into me so too does it, a corona of dark that emanates from his essence. It is cold and dank and hurt. It is loud and clanging and vastness, a vastness full of...

And suddenly, it grows around us, tentacles of blackness enveloping time and space. It has dripped itself over all of the moments in which I have held dominion, it has grabbed my house and dragged it into its house. It has grabbed the souls and minds I've taken by dragging me into it. I do not understand how I can be on the inside and the outside of a man at once but it is so, the shadow, The Heap is vast as all creation and it has eaten it up in its darkness, me included. Brian is shuddering from the belt again and from the breath

A God of Hungry Walls

of the corpse on the back of his neck again and again and again, it has spent so long harming him, so long holding him in its thrall that he has grown used to it though. What it had tried to show me was not the root of this man's pain but that the man carried the pain day in and day out and that every waking moment he has lived with it. It was a warning of sorts.

And I finally know what it is to be the one I could not read or understand. I finally plumb the mystery that I would destroy the world I had built to uncover. I am impossibly small now, curled up in the pocket of something cosmic in scope. And I cannot skitter out. Pressed close to its chest my sole luxury is that I can hear its heartbeat and know its purpose. That purpose? The purpose is pain. The purpose is akin to mine but mine, it ends in having. Is this thing less perfect than I in its machinations? Though it possesses, it too is possessed. Is it really a boon to be used?

I am in a tiny body. I had thought I knew smallness through Antonia, walking whisper. She had seemed so fragile and suggestible, gate and portal oh so very open to assassins and lies and instigators and to treacherous thoughts and misconceptions. She had been, she'd been molded and melted into something that would quietly serve its purpose, practical as a dustpan and broom. I had thought I knew smallness through Kaz's insignificance and need to be coddled and approved of or through shrinking Leah, vanishing fast 'til gone at last. But I have not looked through the wet brown eyes of a child of six living in fear of a giant that might have lurked right outside.

I know streaks of red on someone's back and bruises on the ass. I know what it is to be quiet and behave. This shouldn't make me so mad. This shouldn't make me afraid. I do not like this. Let me out. Let me out. I DO NOT LIKE THIS! LET ME OUT! I DO NOT LIKE THIS! LET ME OUT! I remember this man in the grey suit, with his rotting face and the maggots crawling up and down his face. I'm not afraid of the dead. I'm not afraid of ghosts. My name is Brian Kinney. I'm six. I'm stuck here and I'm scared and I need you to let me out of it.

The man in the grey suit is in here again and dad's been drinking. Mom says when dad's been drinking, he's not responsible for what he does. I don't like that. I want to be mad at him for what he does when he's been drinking. He's going to hit me again when he comes back. I shouldn't have been bad I guess. I don't know what I did but I shouldn't have been bad. I think the man in the grey suit is dead.

"I wasn't the one, I didn't lock you in here, so you can't get out. You'll see sunlight when it's time."

I've heard this before. I know I've heard this before. Where have I heard this before? Am I me again? What are you doing to me? I want out. You did do this to me. I'm stuck in here. Let me out! It's dark and confusing and he's coming up soon. These aren't my thoughts. This isn't me. Mom said there are no such things as monsters and there are no haunted houses. She said it while she was looking right at this thing and I know it was behind me, the great big shadow.

The man in grey is dead and he smells and I don't understand what he's saying to me. When the shadow comes, everybody gets mad and dad starts telling that story again or he locks me in the closet with the dead people and the noises and I just want out. But when I get out, he'll be there with the belt because I was bad and he hopes I'll learn my lesson but nobody tells me what lesson I'm supposed to be learning or why I was bad. Mom tells me that dad isn't responsible for when he's been drinking.

"There will be ways to forget this, and one day, you can make it so you won't have to sit in dark and wait for sunlight. Look back to this and the way out opens up. The world is full of bottles, scalpels, pills."

I've heard this before. He stuck me inside of himself.

154

He stuck me inside of the thing inside of himself. I'm small and afraid and deceived by forces bigger than me. He cannot be bigger than me, he's crossed my threshold, he's still inside me, he still belongs to me. I don't understand how the Closetsong can be his when he belongs to it or I can be his when belongs to me.

"You are mine," says the voice of the Heap, "you are here in the closet with him and there you'll stay. You shouldn't have tried to take from me what was mine."

I pound against the walls of this nightmare, begging to see light I could never see again, borrowing the tiny fists of a child that can't get out, a child with a dusty cadaver breathing down his neck and a father waiting right outside to strike him. To have him is to be had by the Closetsong. I have been tricked. Nothing has ever tricked me. It outrages me. I smash the boy's head against the door but nobody outside it hears. Nobody will let him out. Nobody will let me out. It is slowing down this moment, stretching it so it is all of time, encompassing creation. History, which was a toy to me is now my dungeon, worse even than this closet.

Behind the layers and layers, Antonia is looking into Brian's eyes, eyes that are getting heavy, eyes that are about to close forever. I am inside Brian and Brian is inside the house inside of me as I am inside the closet inside of him. Space and time and mind make no sense. Nothing is making sense to me. I have been tricked. The Closetsong has tricked me. Brian is shivering with torment and blood loss. The closet is hurting him, the Closetsong saps his will and is leaking out his spirit.

Antonia inside of me, inside of him, as I struggle to escape and he struggles to maintain control of the Closetsong is looking at him, tears in her long gone eyes. She doesn't understand. Nobody could. I have been tricked. I have taken this prison and now I am inside it and she wants in. She reaches out her hand.

"I love you, Brian," she says, "you're dying."

"Slowly," he says, "I can't move, I can't do anything but it will almost take forever. I'll hurt like this for a very very long time."

History hurts him as he bleeds out and he refuses the hand of the woman that he loves more than life itself, a hand that would give him comfort if he took it and it could be the start of holding her and touching her forever. If he could hold her and touch her forever, he'd be as good as me, a master of having, a god in the walls of himself. But he turns down her hand and I don't understand why.

"Take her hand!" I hiss at him, pounding on the eternal closet door, "Hold her! Kiss her! Fuck her! She could be yours forever!"

"No!" he says to me, to her.

"I'm not being made to do this," she says, coming closer to him.

"I know."

"So, what do you want me to do?"

Though he is bleeding to death forever and struggling for control of the Closetsong, he manages to take a step. The confused homunculus and Doctorpuppet and Maddy part as he walks, no longer under my control since I have no control. Antonia follows close behind him.

"Where are we going?" she asks him, concerned.

"We're not going anywhere," he says.

I look out through the eyes of the people inside of me and I want to scream. He is shambling with all his fading strength, the strength of a young man dying forever until he can never die again, he is shambling with all his fading strength and he is going to make the front door. The girl who left had come back to me again but she had belonged to me. Though he belongs to me, here in the closet, I belong to him as well and she, the sly bastard, she belongs to him now.

She reaches out to touch him and he pulls away.

"I belong to you," she says, "I'll belong to you forever. I love you."

"I know," he says, "but you don't belong to me."

The closet door is so hard to bang down. I wonder if I bashed his head open and splatted his brains on that invincible door, would he have been dead before I needed to claim him. I am pleading to the Closetsong to let me hurt him more. It hates him so and he is bleeding to death now, and bleeding to death for longer than anyone could actually bleed.

"I don't understand,"says Antonia, "what are you doing? Why did you decide to die for nothing?"

He turns the knob. I shout out through the closet, I try to shout through his mouth, I try to call the homonoculus to stop him before he can open it. But nothing comes up. He is in so much anguish and dying so long, the thing spent so long hurting him.

"You don't belong to me," he says, hands bleeding, pale, his eyes heavy, "you don't belong to me, you belong to you."

"I love you," she says, as if she needed to say it again, as if I didn't feel it in his rapidly emptying veins here in the closet.

He opens the door, turns the knob and she steps out into the light. And suddenly, I'm hurting worse in the vastness of this man's time. I feel something I have never felt before and I cannot fathom it. I have known it in the minds of hearts which I thought I knew fully by having. But you cannot know something fully even by having it. I look in all the things I have and I cannot find this feeling as I know it as mine. I cannot feel it as I feel it as mine.

I had something and now I do not. I treasured it. I valued it and played with it often and tried to know its ways. But I never really did. I am looking for the places when I had her, seeking her out to drag her back and I see now just the image, just the memory. I cannot touch it but I can just remember touching it. She has stepped into the light and she is gone. I slow time for a thousand years I scream at him long as I can fathom long as I can bother and I watch him bleed out long as I can fathom long as I can bother and I need him to know what he has taken from me and show him all the pain he's given me.

I eventually let him bleed out. And he's dead. And he's mine completely.

"I'll defy you forever," he tells me.

"I'll never stop hurting you."

And he doesn't.

**Garrett Cook** Garrett Cook is the Wonderland Book Award Winning author of *Time Pimp* and four other books. He is also an editor, teacher and can make a mean pot of chili. He currently resides in Portland, OR with his collection of vntage fedoras. He's never lived in a house that wasn't haunted.

# deadite press

**"WZMB" Andre Duza** - It's the end of the world, but we're not going off the air! Martin Stone was a popular shock jock radio host before the zombie apocalypse. Then for six months the dead destroyed society. Humanity is now slowly rebuilding and Martin Stone is back to doing what he does best-taking to the airwaves. Host of the only radio show in this new world, he helps organize other survivors. But zombies aren't the only threat. There are others that thought humanity needed to end.

**"Tribesmen" Adam Cesare** - Thirty years ago, cynical sleazeball director Tito Bronze took a tiny cast and crew to a desolate island. His goal: to exploit the local tribes, spray some guts around, cash in on the gore-spattered 80s Italian cannibal craze. But the pissed-off spirits of the island had other ideas. And before long, guts were squirting behind the scenes, as well. While the camera kept rolling...

**"Wet and Screaming" Shane McKenzie** - From a serial killer's yard sale to a hoarder's hideous secret. From a cartoon character made real to a man addicted to car accidents. From a bloody Halloween to child murder as a means for saving the world. The rules of normalcy and society no longer apply - you're now in a place of cruelty, terror, and things that go bump in the night. In Shane McKenzie's first collection - he explores the horrific, the grotesque, the perverse, and the downright bizarre in ten short stories.

**"Suffer the Flesh" Monica J. O'Rourke** - Zoey always wished she was thinner. One day she meets a strange woman who informs her of an ultimate weight-loss program, and Zoey is quickly abducted off the streets of Manhattan and forced into this program. Zoey's enrolling whether she wants to or not. Held hostage with many other women, Zoey is forced into degrading acts of perversion for the amusement of her captors. ...

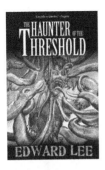

**"The Haunter of the Threshold" Edward Lee -** There is something very wrong with this backwater town. Suicide notes, magic gems, and haunted cabins await her. Plus the woods are filled with monsters, both human and otherworldly. And then there are the horrible tentacles . . . Soon Hazel is thrown into a battle for her life that will test her sanity and sex drive. The sequel to H.P. Lovecraft's The Haunter of the Dark is Edward Lee's most pornographic novel to date!

**"Boot Boys of the Wolf Reich" David Agranoff -** PIt is the summer of 1989 and they spend their days hanging out and having fun, and their nights fighting the local neo-Nazi gangs. Driven back and badly beaten, the local Nazi contingent finds the strangest of allies - The last survivor of a cult of Nazi werewolf assassins. An army of neo-Nazi werewolves are just what he needs. But first, they have some payback for all those meddling Anti-racist SHARPs...

**"The Dark Ones" Bryan Smith -** They are The Dark Ones. The name began as a self-deprecating joke, but it stuck and now it's a source of pride. They're the one who don't fit in. The misfits who drink and smoke too much and stay out all hours of the night. Everyone knows they're trouble. On the outskirts of Ransom, TN is an abandoned, boarded-up house. Something evil happened there long ago. The evil has been contained there ever since, locked down tight in the basement—until the night The Dark Ones set it free . . .

**"Genital Grinder" Ryan Harding -** *"Think you're hardcore? Think again. If you've handled everything Edward Lee, Wrath James White, and Bryan Smith have thrown at you, then put on your rubber parka, spread some plastic across the floor, and get ready for Ryan Harding, the unsung master of hardcore horror. Abandon all hope, ye who enter here. Harding's work is like an acid bath, and pain has never been so sweet."*
- Brian Keene

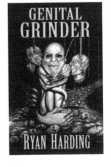

## AVAILABLE FROM AMAZON.COM

CPSIA information can be obtained
at www.ICGtesting.com
Printed in the USA
FSHW010739070620
70977FS